Davis wasn't sure just what had possessed him at that moment. Most likely it was frustration.

O⸗ maybe he just wanted her to back off once and fc all, and the only way he felt he could do that w⸗ to frighten her off. He reasoned he could do th⸗ by kissing her.

V⸗ ich was why he'd turned toward Moira and, o⸗ rating on what amounted to automatic pilot, he su⸗ denly and without a word pulled her to him ⸗ pite her seat belt. He didn't even remember ⸗ ⸗ing against the rather awkward transmission ⸗ t that was between them, dividing them from ⸗ another like an old-fashioned bundling board. ⸗ that he did remember was that he kissed her.

⸗ ssed her hard.

⸗sed her until neither one of them could breathe ⸗ymore and the only sound within the sedan was he one created by two pounding hearts.

* * *

Be sure to check out the next books
in this exciting series:
Cavanaugh Justice—Where Aurora's finest are

CAVANAUGH OR DEATH

BY
MARIE FERRARELLA

First Published in Great Britain 2016
By Mills & Boon, an imprint of HarperCollins*Publishers*
1 London Bridge Street, London, SE1 9GF

© 2016 Marie Rydzynski-Ferrarella

ISBN: 978-0-263-91933-2

18-0416

Our policy is to use papers that are natural, renewable and recyclable products and made from wood grown in sustainable forests.The logging and manufacturing processes conform to the legal environmental regulations of the country of origin.

Printed and bound in Spain
by CPI, Barcelona

USA TODAY bestselling and RITA® Award-winning author **Marie Ferrarella** has written more than two-hundred-and-fifty books for Mills & Boon, some under the name Marie Nicole. Her romances are beloved by fans worldwide. Visit her website, www.marieferrarella.com.

To
Kristin Costello,
With deep appreciation
For being more
Than a nurse.

Prologue

Dawn was beginning to touch the edges of the darkness, hinting that first light was not far away.

Davis Gilroy was only vaguely aware of the time, having glanced at his wristwatch just before entering St. Joseph's Cemetery, the larger of the two cemeteries in the city of Aurora, California, where he had lived all of his life.

Davis assumed that there was a groundskeeper in the area somewhere, possibly grabbing a catnap in one of the three mausoleums on the far end of the property. Or maybe the man was sleeping on the creased brown leather sofa back at the office right off the cemetery's chapel. But other than the groundskeeper, Davis was fairly certain he was the only one in the area.

That was the way he liked it. He liked being alone.

Although he was a detective in the police department's major crime division, Davis wasn't much of a people person. Especially since losing his last two partners, Detective Mike Chan and Detective Ed Ramirez, both of whom now permanently resided at this same cemetery.

But he wasn't here to pay his respects to the two men he had worked beside for a total of less than three years. They were each decent men and good detectives in their own right, though he hadn't socialized with either of them in life and saw no reason to visit them now that the conversation would only be one-sided.

The only people he had one-sided conversations with these days were his parents: James and Martha Gilroy. It was their mutual grave he'd come to visit, as he did at least once a month, more often if he got the chance. For the most part his life consisted of work and sleep—and work kept him pretty busy. Coming here was his only deviation from that narrow path.

Davis stood in front of the double headstone. It was a wide, expensive marble piece that had taken him months to save up for—putting aside every cent he could out of his paychecks—until the tombstone was finally paid off and in place over his parents' grave instead of the meager one his uncle had put there.

They were together in death just as they had been in life. His father had taken pride in the fact that it had been love at first sight for both of them. As he'd gotten older, Davis had pretended not to listen, though he'd never tired of hearing the details.

He'd been almost thirteen the day they died. They

had been together in the car that Sunday, but only he had survived.

That still haunted him.

Davis was kneeling over their grave, the bouquet of fresh white roses—his mother's favorite—placed just beneath the headstone. Spring had been part of the terrain for a good month. His mother had always loved spring.

He felt the sting of tears smart at the corners of his eyes and was glad no one was around to see him.

Here, alone with his parents, away from other inquisitive eyes, he was free to be himself the way he wasn't in his daily life. Six-foot-two, thirty-four-year-old men didn't get emotional or shed tears about events that had happened more than two decades ago.

But there was no one here to judge him.

"Sorry I haven't been around lately—had a case that wasn't easy to solve. But I'm here now and that's what counts, right, Dad?"

His father had never bothered berating him for time that had been lost; he'd only pointed out that there was time ahead to be used—until there wasn't any time ahead left.

"Can you believe it?" Davis asked, addressing the two people beneath the tombstone. "It's been almost twenty-one years now. Twenty-one years since you and Mom relocated here."

That was as specific as he allowed himself to get, even when "talking" with the two people who had been ripped out of his life by that fatal car accident. An accident that had taken them from him and subsequently thrust him in with his father's older brother, John. Being the only family member he had left, John had begrudgingly taken him in.

The reluctance had faded when John—Davis could never bring himself to call him Uncle John because that was far too warm a title for a man who never smiled, never asked him how he was doing—had discovered that there was a substantial insurance policy to be held in trust for his nephew until his eighteenth birthday. His father had named John the executor of the trust.

John had turned out to be a rather resourceful man when it came to finding ways to siphon off some of that trust fund money to pay for the "expenses" involved in raising an orphan from the age of thirteen to eighteen. It eventually came to light that John had taken advantage of every loophole he could find or fabricate.

There was a coldness in John's house that never abated; a coldness that seemed to set the tone for the rest of his own young life. Davis never felt any resentment toward his father's older brother. He never felt anything at all. All he had wanted from the moment he had entered the man's house was the freedom to leave it. That freedom came on his eighteenth birthday.

He'd taken whatever money was left in the insurance policy—precious little—and put it toward his education, becoming what his father had been before him: a cop. But first his father had wanted him to get his college degree. It was the only stipulation his father had ever placed on him.

"I miss you guys, but then, you already know that,

don't you?" Davis murmured. He sighed. "Well, I just wanted to come by, make sure that they're keeping the weeds off your plot and—"

Davis stopped abruptly, certain that he'd heard a noise out of place in the eerie quiet that enshrouded the cemetery at this hour.

Cocking his head in the direction of the sound, he listened closely.

Intently.

Davis could have sworn it was the sound of a shovel accidentally hitting stone.

At this hour? Nobody buried anyone before the sun came up.

Either his imagination had gotten the better of him, or—

"Later," he promised the pair who remained eternally young, eternally smiling, in his mind. "Something sounds off. You know what I mean, Dad."

And with that Detective First Class Davis Gilroy silently hurried in the direction he could have sworn he'd heard something out of keeping with the sleepy rhythm of the cemetery.

When it came to hunches, Davis was hardly ever wrong.

The next moment, as he turned a corner, he thought he saw something moving in the shadows.

Two somethings moving in the shadows.

As he gained ground, zigzagging and sprinting around headstones, Davis realized that the shadows were actually people. Two people, dressed entirely in black. Black pullovers, black slacks, black boots and black ski masks pulled down over their faces.

They looked like second-story cat burglars—except that they were here in a cemetery, hovering around one of the tombstones.

"Hey, you!" Davis called out. "Stop!"

The two dark figures did the exact opposite.

They bolted.

Chapter 1

Every morning, halfway through her run, Moira Cavanaugh asked herself the same question: Why am I doing this?

The answer she'd arrived at some time ago, and that still held as of this morning, was that if she *didn't* put her running shoes on, throw on a sweatshirt and shorts, then pound on the pavement for a good hour, she would be moving around at half speed for the rest of the day. Not to mention that she'd spend the rest of the day feeling guilty for slacking off. Because of what she did for a living, she needed to be at the top of her game all day, *every* day.

So here she was, a police detective like most of the rest of her vast, sprawling clan, sweating and breathing progressively harder in the predawn light, counting off the seconds until she was nearing the end of this self-inflicted torture. And fervently wishing that she was more like her older brother, Malloy, who rolled out of bed, hit the ground running, was bright-eyed and bushy-tailed by the time he drove into the Aurora Police Department parking lot.

But she wasn't like Malloy. To be in peak condition, she needed to jump-start her day, and running seemed to be the only thing that accomplished that for her. Varying her route caused her to remain wide-awake instead of merely going through the motions.

By choosing a different route each morning—one of ten or so she'd marked down for herself—she had to stay alert to take the right path home. She only had twenty minutes once her run was over to get ready and be in the car, on her way to work.

The only thing Moira hated more than being sluggish was being late.

Jogging first thing in the morning before she was even fully awake kept both from happening—even though it felt like hell while she was doing it.

This morning's route was the creepy route—especially since the street lamp in front of the cemetery had picked today to go out and there was only a half-moon up in the sky to guide her past the tall, imposing, black wrought-iron gates.

Cemeteries didn't bother her in the light of day, but there was almost a sinister vibe about them before the sun came up.

However, this was the route she'd drawn out of the candy dish where she kept all the routes she'd picked to run. Being guided by the luck of the draw was another way she had of combating monotony.

"Just a little farther, Moy, just a little farther," she mumbled, egging herself on. "You can do this. You've done it before, you'll do it again. Pay no attention to the eerie place on your left. It's just your imagination, you know that."

Her imagination and the ghost stories Malloy had loved telling her every night when their ages were both still in the single digits.

"Just keep on running. There're no such things as ghosts or creatures that go bump in the night, just Malloy, doing his best to scare you. Think about something else."

His best, back then, had always been more than good enough and it had laid the foundation for the uneasy wariness she experienced whenever she passed a cemetery after twilight.

Logically, the fear had no foundation. Emotionally, though, was another story entirely.

Emotionally, it was—

Moira's breath caught in her throat.

There were two shadowy figures racing out of the cemetery—and they looked as if they were running right toward her.

Moira jumped out of the way, just in case they actually *were* running toward her, but the evasive maneuver only managed to complicate matters.

One of the shadowy figures slammed right into her, knocking the air out of her.

Her imagination going full blast, Moira had half

expected the shadowy figure to go right through her, but it hadn't.

And now that she thought about it, the figure had felt very solid for a ghost.

She watched, stunned, as the "ghost" scrambled to its feet and then proceeded to run off despite the limp it seemed to have acquired from the collision.

The shadowy figures just kept on going as if she hadn't been there.

Maybe to them she wasn't.

"Hey!" she cried, rattled and stunned as well as beginning to lose her temper. The notion that the duo were ghosts had quickly disappeared. Nothing that hit so hard upon collision was made of vapor and air. She had definitely been hit by a flesh-and-blood human being. It frustrated her that she was unable to specify anything beyond that vague description.

Because of the fact that both running figures had been covered in black from head to foot, she couldn't have even identified the gender of either.

The next second she saw the reason that the duo had come flying out of the cemetery. They were being chased by someone.

Him she could make out.

He was a tall, dark-blond haired man who ran with both the grace and speed of a professional athlete. He'd appeared to be gaining on the slower of the two shadowy figures until he'd seen her sprawled out on the pavement.

The thought that she'd had more graceful moments flashed through Moira's mind.

Stopping for a second, the dour-looking stranger put his hand out to her. Her ego bruised, Moira accepted his help. There was a time for pride and a time for practicality. This was one of those latter times.

"You okay?" he asked in a resonant voice as he pulled her to her feet.

"Yes."

She was about to add a coda that it actually depended on his definition of "okay" since her unexpected sudden meeting with the pavement had jarred her to the roots of her teeth, but Moira never got the opportunity.

The blond stranger was off and running after the duo in less time than it took for her words to form in her head.

Dusting herself off, Moira stared after the stranger's departing figure, no longer able to see the two he was chasing and trying to overtake. They'd had too much of a head start on him.

It seemed as if everyone was in top physical form, she thought grudgingly. The next moment the chivalrous, silent stranger disappeared from her view.

Moira sighed. Maybe all this was just a figment of her bored imagination, but somehow she strongly doubted it.

At this point dawn was laying the finishing touches for its dramatic entrance, turning up the light around the edges of the visible world and then multiplying that light and spreading it around the surrounding area.

Moira turned and looked at the entrance to the cemetery. It no longer appeared like the scene of countless ghost stories waiting to be told—or lived—just a place where people brought their loved ones so the latter could have a final resting place.

Moira regarded the cemetery thoughtfully.

Just what was the big deal in the cemetery at this hour of the morning, anyway? The duo that had run right over her certainly seemed as if they could belong to a cult, but that wasn't true of the man who had helped her to her feet then took off before she could thank him.

Could he have been the night watchman or maybe the groundskeeper?

Curious, Moira glanced at her watch. If she ran at her best top speed to her condo, she could make it in twelve minutes. That left her about five to investigate whatever had been going on in the cemetery—if there actually *had* been something going on.

She regarded the grounds beyond the arched entrance.

That was an awful lot of territory to cover in five minutes. Still, mysteries of any kind had always intrigued her. She couldn't resist.

Running in and moving fast, Moira managed to take in close to a quarter of the area. Scanning it, nothing caught her attention.

Maybe the duo had been just kids dressed in black to blend into the night as they explored the cemetery. Maybe they were doing it on a dare.

A lot of stupid things were done in the name of a dare.

If the blond stranger *was* a security guard—or a groundskeeper—then he'd been chasing them off.

She turned to leave the cemetery when something caught her eye. Aware of the seconds ticking by, Moira still felt compelled to investigate. It was in her DNA, not just because she was a Cavanaugh, but because she was part of the police department's understaffed robbery division.

Moving closer, she realized what it was that had set off her alarm.

One of the headstones in the vicinity looked as if it had been knocked over and then righted again—but not all that well. The stone was tilted.

Stepping even closer, Moira read the writing on the headstone. "'Emily Jenkins, beloved wife of Hal Jenkins.'" It also gave the year of her birth and her death. Whoever Emily Jenkins was, she had been buried a couple of months more than twenty years.

Moira regarded the list of the headstone. Maybe it was just due to regular shifting of the earth. After all, this was California. Some areas moved more than others. If there had been regular minor tremors or just simple shifting, that could have made the headstone move and lean as if it had had one too many.

Reaching out, Moira touched the headstone. She immediately saw that it was not only listing, it was downright loose. That took effort.

Human effort.

Could the people who had knocked her down been grave robbers?

Grave robbers? Moira, this is Aurora. Nobody even touches a headstone if they can help it.

Yet what other explanation could there be? This needed further examination—but not at this moment, Moira sternly reminded herself. She had someplace to be.

Taking off from the cemetery to avoid being late to work, Moira made herself a promise to come back as soon as she could today to investigate the scene thoroughly.

Emily Jenkins had been violated—or at least her grave had.

What she needed to find out was why.

Moira made it back to her home in what amounted to a new record, at least for her. Her lungs were near bursting as she shed her clothes all the way to the shower, littering the floor with them.

Jumping into the glass enclosure, she turned on the water before she had even securely locked the shower door. Five very swift minutes later she was toweling herself dry, leaving tiny pools of water to mark her path to her closet.

She had no time for breakfast or the life-affirming coffee she usually swore by. Instead, dressed, Moira was back out on the pavement less than twelve minutes after she had first inserted her key into her condo's front door.

She hoped she could find something edible and at least vaguely nutritious in the vending machines at the station. She had her doubts.

Pulling into the station's rear parking lot, Moira could have sworn she saw someone who vaguely reminded her of the dark-blond stranger who had helped her to her feet.

At least, he resembled the man from the rear, which was the only view she had at the moment. Tall, dark blond and broad shoulders, he *could* have been the stranger from the cemetery.

Or, more likely, just another private citizen coming to the station to lodge a complaint or to respond to a call from one of the many police detectives inhabiting the building.

Her curiosity still on high alert, Moira quickened her pace in an attempt to catch up with the blond stranger.

He entered the building before she did. Moira stepped up her pace again.

As she got into the building, she discovered that not only should she have quickened her pace, she should have increased it to a sprint. The stranger she was trying so hard to get a better look at was nowhere to be seen.

"Must have caught an elevator," she told herself under her breath.

It was either that or accept the explanation that the stranger had vanished into thin air. She preferred the elevator.

"You know, they say the mind's the first to go for some police detectives. Of course, that's assuming that they *have* a mind to lose, which, in your case, the jury is still out about."

Moira didn't have to turn around to know who was talking to her. But she'd learned a long time ago that ignoring her brother and pretending he wasn't there didn't make him go away. If anything, it just made Malloy up his ante.

With a sigh, she turned around to face him. "I see that someone woke up on the right side of the bed this morning." The smile she forced to her lips looked deliberately phony by all accounts.

The grin on the tall, handsome detective's face was, according to more than half the female population, incredibly enticing.

"Actually, little sister," he told her with a wicked wink, "it was on the right side of the lovely Patricia Morgan, but why quibble over words?"

"Why indeed?" Moira asked crisply, striding toward the elevator quickly.

She knew there was no losing her brother, but for the sake of the game, she had to look as if she at least tried.

"Hey, you okay?" Malloy asked, catching her by the shoulder to take a closer look at her face. "You look like someone rode you hard and put you away wet," he observed seriously.

Moira pulled away from him, although her expression never changed. "Ah, you're as golden-tongued as always, big brother. I can see why all the ladies find you so terribly charming. You obviously have to beat them off with a stick."

"Seriously, Moira, you all right?" Malloy asked. "The back of your head is partially damp. Are you trying for some sort of a new style, or did they turn off your electricity while you were in the middle of blow-drying your hair?"

This time Moira frowned. She hated when he started being too observant when it came to her. "You're the detective, you tell me."

Malloy arched a bemused eyebrow. "Since when has anyone ever been able to tell you anything?" he called after her as Moira walked into the elevator.

"I always listen to someone who makes sense," she replied innocently, then added, "I guess that leaves you out, doesn't it?" just as the elevator doors closed, taking her away from his view.

Only when the doors were securely closed did Moira reach behind her head and touch the back of her hair—and frowned.

Damn, she thought, annoyance nibbling away at her. Malloy was right. For some reason, in her hurry to get to the precinct on time, she had somehow neglected to dry the length of hair right in the middle.

She briefly thought about going into the bathroom and making unorthodox use of the hand-dryer, but shrugged away the idea.

With luck, no one would look in her direction until that section of her hair air-dried itself.

Right now she had something more important on her mind, Moira reminded herself as she reached her floor. She wanted to tell her lieutenant about the suspicious scene she'd stumbled across at the cemetery.

Much as she hated being restrained, she knew that she needed his blessings before she could begin to investigate.

Chapter 2

Before getting down to the business at hand, Moira paused in the break room long enough to get a cup of what passed for coffee in the precinct. It was universally agreed that the quality was poor, but at least the coffee was hot. In addition, it was also extremely bitter. The combination definitely revved up her engine and put her in a fast-forward mode.

Fortified and sufficiently jolted into a keenly alert state, Moira placed what was left of the black swill on her desk and marched herself into her superior's small, glass-enclosed office.

Legend had it that Lieutenant Jacob Carver had once been a passably decent-looking man. Years on the force had etched themselves into his jowl-lined face, giving him what appeared to be a permanent hangdog frown, accented by scowling, bushy eyebrows that came close to meeting over the bridge of his patrician nose; all of which looked more than mildly intimidating to most newly minted detectives assigned to his squad.

Although Moira didn't welcome interaction with the less-than-jovial man, she wasn't intimidated by him, either. Growing up in a family of seven, most of which had excelled in rowdiness before they had reached the age of three, had given her a spine of steel and a sense of self that served Moira quite well in her chosen field. She was polite, and deferred to higher authority when she had to, but she was never intimidated.

The door to Carver's office was closed. He wasn't—and never had been—an open-door kind of superior. If a subordinate wanted an audience with the man, they had to follow a number of rules—the first of which was knocking before entering. The second of which was to be invited in before entering.

Moira paused to knock and then, not waiting for an invitation, she opened the lieutenant's door. "Got a minute, Lieutenant?"

"Got sixty of them in every hour," he responded without looking up from the report he was currently writing.

Since Carver hadn't said no, Moira took that as an invitation by default and proceeded to enter the man's inner sanctum.

"I'd like to run something past you," she told the man, closing the door behind her.

Ordinarily she would have just left it open, but she knew that Carver was incredibly secretive about every conversation he had with anyone, especially any of his people. It didn't matter about what. He liked maintaining an air of secrecy.

Carver ignored her for a moment, undoubtedly with the hope that she would simply go away. But everyone in the precinct had come to realize that the name Cavanaugh was synonymous with stubbornness and, though it irritated him, he'd learned that the one assigned to his division was no exception.

So when Moira remained inside the room, he sighed, put down his pen—a holdout of a bygone era, Carver still liked to use pen and paper rather than keyboard and mouse—and looked up.

"And what is it that you want to run past me, Cavanaugh?" he asked wearily.

Moira had long since decided not to take offense at the way Carver uttered her surname. There were Cavanaughs in every department of the precinct and, while most of the police personnel were on friendly terms with them, there were others who were not. The resentful ones believed that the Cavanaugh name instantly bought those who wore it a certain amount of leeway and gave them access to shortcuts that other officers and detectives were not privy to.

Carver was on the fence when it came to buying into that philosophy.

She could, however, detect the resentment in her lieutenant's voice whenever he said her last name in a tone that sounded as if he was partially taunting her. Such as now.

"When I was out for my run this morning—" Moira started.

As she began to answer his question, Carver reached for a powdered-sugar-dusted cruller, one of two that he always picked up every morning on his way to the precinct. He paused for a moment, giving her a dark look as if she'd thrown the line in to mock him and the pear-like shape his body had taken on over the years.

"Oh, yeah, I forgot. You're big on health, aren't you?"

The look in Carver's brown eyes challenged her as he bit into his cruller with a vengeance. Powdered sugar rained down on the page he'd been writing on, but he seemed not to notice.

"It wakes me up," Moira replied matter-of-factly. She wasn't about to get sucked into a debate about the pros and cons of what she did in her private life. "Anyway, as I passed by St. Joseph's Cemetery entrance—"

Carver stopped eating. "You run past the cemetery?" he asked incredulously. "Maybe you should transfer to Homicide if you like dead people so much."

Moira had no idea how the man managed to make the leap from what she was telling him by way of background information to what he'd just said, but again, she detected the antagonistic note in his voice and didn't rise to the bait.

"I like being on this squad just fine, sir," she replied. "Anyway, these two figures—"

"Figures?" he questioned skeptically. "You mean, like, zombies?" It was clear that he was mocking her and not about to take anything she said seriously unless she forced him to acknowledge it in that light.

"No. Like, robbers, sir," Moira corrected matter-of-factly, doing her best to get to her point and not be sidetracked by his interjections. "They were dressed in black and wearing ski masks. One of them ran right into me and just kept going—"

Carver dusted off his hands and reached for the crumpled napkin in the bag that contained the crullers. "I'm guessing there's a point to this ghost story, Detective."

"There is, sir. I went into the cemetery to find out why the two figures were fleeing—"

He eyed her impatiently. "Let me guess, Dracula was after them."

She hadn't wanted to mention this until she'd gotten Carver to agree to let her investigate the tampered-with gravesite. "No, as a matter of fact, there was some blond guy running after them—"

"Ah, the plot thickens," Carver mocked. "Does this 'blond guy' have a name?"

"I'm sure he does, sir, but he ran by too fast for me to ask him," she said, now impatiently trying to get to her point.

"Too bad, this sounded like it might have gotten interesting." Carver looked wistfully at the second cruller but apparently decided to wait until he was alone again before having it. "Is there a point to this haunting little tale, Cavanaugh?"

"I went into the cemetery and saw that one of the

headstones had been disturbed. I think—as strange as it might sound—that they were trying to rob a grave."

Carver stared at her as if she'd lost her mind. Certainly she'd lost his interest, mild as it had been to begin with. "And you want to do what about that?"

Moira squared her shoulders defensively a little bit as she said, "I'd like permission to investigate the site so I can see if they were trying to dig something up."

Carver's frown deepened. To his way of thinking, he had likely indulged the detective way too long. It was obvious that he wanted her out of his office and out of his thinning hair. "In case it has escaped your attention, Cavanaugh, this is the *robbery* division."

"I know that, sir," Moira answered evenly, painfully aware that shouting at the man would get her nowhere except reprimanded—if not suspended. "Grave robbing would fall under that heading."

"Grave robbing," he repeated, clearly stunned.

This wasn't going well but Carver, despite all his foibles, was, at bottom, a decent detective, or had been before he'd assumed command of Robbery. That was the part of him she was attempting to reach.

"Yes, sir."

His eyes narrowed as he pinned her in place. "Who complained?"

Moira wasn't sure what he was getting at. "Excuse me, sir?"

"Who complained?" he repeated evenly before spelling it out for her. "In order to go out and investigate this so-called 'headstone disturbance' we need to have someone file a complaint."

The lieutenant was crossing his t's and dotting his i's. He only did that when it served his purpose—or he didn't want to okay something. She knew for a fact the man bent rules when he wanted to.

Playing along, she said, "Okay, I'll file."

Carver sighed dramatically. "Didn't anyone in that family of yours teach you anything, Cavanaugh? *You* can't be the one to file a complaint. In this case, as you've laid it out, you're a jogger, not an interested party."

"But I'm very interested," she persisted, picking up on the word he'd used. "What if there's a cult of grave robbers out there?"

"In Aurora?" he mocked. Growing just the slightest bit serious, Carver added, "Then we would have heard about it."

"Maybe they're just getting started," Moira countered.

Carver eyed her in moody silence for several seconds, weighing options. "You're not going to drop this, are you?"

Her first reaction was to say no but she squelched it. Knowing better than to go up against the lieutenant outright, Moira tried to approach the subject in a calm, logical manner. "I really think there's something to this, Lieutenant."

"Of course you do." Carver swallowed the curse that rose to his lips. He paused for a long moment, as if weighing the pros and cons of her request. "Okay. I'm a reasonable man," he told her.

The jury's still out on that, Moira couldn't help thinking.

"Go and investigate your heart out—just you, not your partner," he clarified, adding, "Warner's got real police work to do."

Moira had always maintained that she could get along with anyone, even the devil, but there was something about Detective Alfred Warner that made her wish she had another partner instead of the older, by-the-book detective.

Maybe it was because the man reminded her too much of Carver.

Whatever the reason, she was more than happy to investigate whatever was going on at the cemetery on her own. She wondered if the man realized that.

"Yes, sir," she replied.

"Talk to the cemetery caretaker," Carver suggested. "Find out if he knows anything or has noticed anything funny going on. See if this has happened before. But if you can't find anything—and I'm talking something tangible here—in forty-eight hours, that's it. I don't want to hear any more about it. Forty-eight hours, that's your window, Cavanaugh. Understood?"

"Understood, sir," she quickly responded. "And thank you, sir."

It was obvious from the expression on his face that he was far from happy about this, but he didn't want to just arbitrarily ignore what she'd brought him just in case there *was* something to it.

"Yeah, yeah." Carver waved her away. "Just get

out of my office. And close the door behind you," he added sharply.

"I always do, sir," she responded with a smile as she gripped the doorknob.

She thought she heard Carver mutter something caustic under his breath as she left, but she knew better than to ask what. Pretending she hadn't heard his voice, she closed the door behind her.

As she paused by her desk to make a notation on her computer, she glanced up to see that her partner had just walked in and was approaching his desk.

The next moment he was removing his jacket and draping the twenty-year-old article of clothing over the back of his chair.

Glancing over toward her, he asked suspiciously, "Who brightened your day?"

She was not about to waste any time going into specifics. Warner had a habit of taking everything apart and down to the tiniest component. Opting for brevity, Moira simply said, "The lieutenant just gave me a case to look into."

Warner dropped into his chair. The fifteen pounds he had gained on the job in the past year caused the chair to creak loudly in protest.

"Hell, I've already got too much to do," he complained.

"This is just a solo case, Warner," she told him cheerfully. "Nothing for you to worry about."

Which, once the words were out, she knew was exactly what Warner was about to do since she wasn't giving him any details. The detective was not keen on exerting more effort than he possibly had to, but neither did he like being purposely excluded from anything.

Moira admitted to herself that it was small of her to bait him this way, but she had heard the man say several nasty things not just about her but about others in her family. It had been all she could do to hold her tongue when she did.

Making the man feel as if he was missing out on something was, in her estimation, merely a small payback.

"See you later," she told him cheerfully as she walked away, heading toward the doorway.

"Wait, what's this case about?" Warner called after her.

Moira pretended she didn't hear the question and just kept walking.

Her smile widened. Maybe she was being petty, but as far as she was concerned, Warner deserved it. She couldn't ask for another partner—there had to be a specific reason for the request and saying that the man annoyed her just wouldn't fly with the lieutenant—so she had to satisfy herself with this.

Besides, according to her father, this was the kind of thing that built character. Had she actually said anything to her father, he would have advised her to stick it out with Warner.

"I'm going to have one hell of a character by the time that man retires," she mumbled to herself as she pressed for the elevator. "If I survive," she added in an even softer whisper.

Moira glanced around to see if anyone was nearby

who might have overheard her monologue, but although there were a few people in the hallway, no one appeared to be in close hearing range.

She would have to watch herself, Moira silently chided. She talked to herself far too often. She didn't want anyone thinking, or worse, *saying*, that she was crazy.

The elevator still hadn't arrived. Impatient, Moira pressed on the down button a second time.

Where *was* that damn elevator, anyway?

It seemed to her that the thing ran slower and slower every day. She was anxious to get going before Carver suddenly changed his mind and had someone come after her so he could tell her to drop her yet-to-begin investigation.

Now that she had gotten the green light to investigate the scene at the cemetery, she intended to make the most of it, especially since she was flying solo.

She could tell by Carver's expression that he hadn't thought there was anything to her hunch. But she did. She was a Cavanaugh and she had yet to meet a single one of her extended clan who didn't believe in hunches or rely on them heavily when push came to shove.

The elevator *still* hadn't made an appearance.

Annoyed—and growing more so—Moira glanced up to see that according to what was registering above the elevator doors, the car was still on the sixth floor, where it had been for at least the past three minutes.

What if it was broken again? The elevator had been out of commission for half a day last Tuesday. And before that it had been down for the better part of two days about a month ago.

Giving up, Moira went to the stairwell. Good exercise anyway.

The heavy door shut behind her as she entered the stairwell. Her hand was on the banister when she heard the sharp staccato of a pair of men's shoes hitting the metal steps.

Obviously someone else had lost patience with the elevator, too, she thought, glancing overhead to where the sound of quickening footsteps was coming from.

Her mouth dropped open as, for the second time that morning, she found herself looking at the blond stranger from the cemetery.

Chapter 3

As she stood there, with the fire door closed at her back, Moira watched the blond stranger quickly make his way to the next staircase. Dressed exactly the same way as when he'd helped her to her feet outside the cemetery, the stranger appeared to take no notice of her as he headed down the stairs.

"Hey, you!" Moira called out, stunned that he'd made no acknowledgment whatsoever that he wasn't alone in the stairwell. "Wait!"

Apparently the man had hoped to just keep going. However, since she was the only other person in the stairwell, surely he realized she was trying to get his attention.

He paused for a moment midway down the stairs

and was obviously waiting for her to either say something or to ask him a question.

"What are you doing here?" Moira asked, cutting the distance between them quickly. If the man from the cemetery was surprised to see her or even recognized her, Moira noted that he gave no such indication.

"Going down the stairs," he noted with minimal inflection. "Same as you, would be my guess."

Was he being funny or didn't he understand the gist of her question? Upon closer scrutiny, he looked too intelligent to be dumb, so her guess leaned toward the former, even if his expression remained dour.

"I meant in the precinct." Her mind gravitated back to the cemetery and to what Carver had said about needing someone to sign a complaint regarding the headstone being disturbed. Was *that* what he was doing here? "Are you registering a complaint?" she asked. It seemed a logical explanation for his being there, although not why he was in the stairwell.

There was no inflection in his voice as the stranger responded, "Not unless you intend to do something complaint-worthy."

Was he deliberately drawing this out or had she just misjudged him, after all, and he was just being obtuse? She tried again.

"Then why are you in the building?"

The attractive, breathless woman asked an awful lot of questions considering that they didn't know one another, Davis thought.

"Well, for one thing, they pay me to be here."

He watched as her eyebrows pulled together in bewilderment beneath her blond bangs.

"Wait—you work here?"

"Yes."

Moira regarded the stranger suspiciously, once again reevaluating him. He was having fun at her expense, she decided. The man probably was used to getting by on his good looks. Well, that wasn't going to fly with her. "Doing what?" she asked.

A slight, whimsical expression passed over his almost immobile face. "As much or as little as they want me to."

"You're a cop."

"You'd make a hell of a contestant on one of those quiz shows. Me, I don't have any patience for that kind of thing. So," he concluded, calling an end to the unofficial interrogation session, "if you're finished asking questions—"

Moira took another two steps down, putting herself directly into his path and temporarily blocking his escape. "You were the guy chasing those two people at the cemetery, weren't you?"

He stifled a sigh. "Obviously you're not finished asking questions. *Why* are you asking questions?" he asked, pinning her with a glare meant to put her in her place.

"Because, to begin with, I'm not usually run over at six thirty in the morning—" she began.

He cut her off, pointing out the obvious. "I didn't run you over."

"No, but you were chasing the people who did," she

reminded him. "Why were you chasing them?" Had he caught them in the act of grave robbing or was there another reason he had been after them?

He hesitated.

She wouldn't know that it was Davis's habit to play it close to the vest and never reveal too much, even when the one doing the questioning was a bright-eyed, eager blonde his father might have described as being very "easy on the eyes."

"Let's just say that I had a couple of questions of my own for them," he answered simply.

"Like why they were disturbing a gravesite?" she asked pointedly.

He watched her for a long, hard moment and Moira felt as if this cop—if he really *was* one—was looking right into her head.

She didn't care for the way that made her feel.

"What would you know about that?" he finally asked her.

"Nothing," Moira admitted, "which is why I'm asking questions."

He didn't look as if he believed her. The man had the ability to make her want to squirm even though she was telling the truth. Only her mother used to be able to do that, Moira thought in grudging admiration. It took effort to meet his stare and not give any indication of what she was feeling.

"But you knew the gravesite was disturbed." He said it like an accusation.

Moira refused to let him get to her. Instead she pretended she was talking to an uncooperative witness.

"Because after you helped me to my feet," she told him matter-of-factly, "I went into the cemetery to see what was going on that would make three people come tearing out of there."

She watched his rugged, handsome face grow stern.

"You make it sound as if I was with them. I wasn't. I was trying to find out the same thing," he informed her somewhat grudgingly.

She could see that getting information out of this man would be just like pulling teeth—that only made her more determined to get it.

"So you don't know what they were doing there?" she persisted.

He shook his head. "Not a clue."

Moira paused for a moment, debating whether or not to say anything further.

Until a couple of minutes ago she was more than happy to be investigating this possible grave robbery on her own, but it never hurt to have another set of eyes on the subject. And the blond stranger's eyes were a really intriguing shade of blue; a perfect complement to his dark blond, somewhat shaggy hair.

Moira made up her mind.

"Want to find out?" she asked him. When he didn't answer immediately, she decided he probably thought she was putting him on, so she went on to try to convince him to join forces.

"My lieutenant's giving me forty-eight hours to figure out why someone would be messing with a grave at the cemetery. I could use some help. Two sets of eyes are always better than one," she added quickly, hoping that would convince him to agree to join her.

"I don't work in your division," he pointed out evenly.

Moira waved away the observation. "That's no problem. Detectives get loaned out and cross department lines all the time. I could put in a request with your lieutenant—"

"Captain," he corrected.

Moira never lost a beat. "With your captain," she said, "and ask him to allow you to help me with the investigation."

"What would you say was your reason?" he asked, then challenged, "Why would you need my help over someone else's, say, like, in your own department?"

She had an answer ready for that, as well. "I could tell him that you were there at the time, that you think you saw something—"

Davis cut her off. "I saw the same thing that you did."

Why was he fighting her on this? Didn't he *want* to investigate these potential grave robbers? And if he didn't, why didn't he? Was there something here she was missing?

"Still," she continued, "you were in the cemetery at the same time they were—and you chased after them, causing them to flee the premises, possibly before they could finish doing whatever it was they were doing." The more she talked, the more she sold herself on the idea, growing excited at the same time. "So, what do you say?" she asked brightly.

His was not the face of a man who had been won over, Moira couldn't help noticing.

"I say that I don't even know who the hell you are."

"Well, that's easy enough to fix." She put her hand out. "I'm Detective Moira Cavanaugh, robbery division."

He made no effort to take her hand. Instead he repeated her name. "Cavanaugh."

Moira dropped her hand. She knew adversity when she saw it. "One of the many."

She attempted to read his expression and found it utterly impossible. It was like trying to guess at the thoughts of a glass of water. Was he one of the ones on the force who outright resented her because of her name? She would like to believe that if he was, something in his eyes would give his feelings away. Disdain. Annoyance. *Something.*

But he didn't flinch. Didn't look down his nose at her. Didn't reel off his list of imagined Cavanaugh offenses.

All he'd done was repeat her name.

So she tried again. "So, what do you say?"

He appeared unmoved. "I say that there's probably nothing to investigate."

"How can you be sure?" she asked. Then she qualified her question, aware that what she'd say would probably get to him. "Unless, of course, you're the one who disturbed the grave and those two characters in black surprised *you* at it."

She watched the man's face as she delivered her last guess. But there was no telltale look to give him away.

Damn but he was a hard nut to crack.

"Anyone ever tell you that you have a wild imagination?" he asked her.

Well, at least she'd gotten a reaction out of him, Moira thought. "If cops didn't have wild imaginations, half the crimes wouldn't be solved. Thinking outside the box is what does it."

"There's thinking outside the box and then there's thinking outside the whole house," he countered.

It was easy to see which he thought she was guilty of.

"You still haven't given me an answer," she pointed out, crossing her fingers as she asked, "Want to partner up for this?"

"No," he replied flatly.

What Moira couldn't possibly know was that the last thing he wanted was a partner. He'd lost two, not to mention both his parents, and at this point, he felt that bad luck always followed in his wake, striking down anyone he interacted with. He and everyone else would be better off if he just remained a loner, the way he was.

The man on the staircase had aroused her curiosity to a higher level, but even so, Moira knew she couldn't force him to be her partner. Nor could she get him to answer all the questions that were, even now, popping up and multiplying in her head.

"Why?" she asked. "Tell me. Please." Getting answers would have to be done with finesse, but only if she could get this man to talk to her on a regular basis—which she could, but only if they partnered up.

The old saying about leading a horse to water but not being able to make him drink ran through her head.

"My answer is just no," he replied.

Now what?

Moira took a conscious, figurative step back and shrugged. "Your loss, Detective...?" She let her voice trail off, waiting for him to fill in a name.

Instead he replied, "That is a matter of opinion."

He hadn't responded the way she'd hoped he would. The man just didn't know how to play the game, she thought, frustrated.

Or maybe he did but just refused to.

Moira took one more stab at it. "Oh c'mon, you've *got* to have a name."

"Yes, I do."

For just the tiniest split second she entertained the idea of justifiable homicide. Then, taking a deep breath, she asked, "So what is it?"

If nothing else, the woman had succeeded in making him curious as to how far she was going to go with this. "There's no reason for you to know."

"Detective," she said, a slight edge working its way into her voice, "there're just the two of us in this stairwell and accidents can happen at any place, any time."

Disciplined restraint kept him from laughing at her. "I'm no expert, but my guess is that I outweigh you by a good fifty pounds."

She was one step below him and from this vantage point, he towered over her. Moira Cavanaugh didn't give an inch as a fire came into her eyes. "The first rule of martial arts is using your opponent's weight against them."

To Moira's surprise, she heard a dry laugh escape the detective's lips.

"You really are determined to get your own way, aren't you?" he asked her. "Let me guess, you're an only child who was always indulged."

Boy, did he have the wrong number. "I'm one of seven who had to fight her way to the top each and every time. *Nobody* indulged *anybody* in my family," she informed him proudly.

There was no point in his telling her that she wasn't the only one trained in martial arts—his parents had signed him up for classes to help build his confidence because he had been small for his age and had been picked on in school. What he'd learned at that very young age had helped him hold more than his own in life.

He regarded her in prolonged silence, then, just as she appeared ready to walk away, said, "I'll talk to my captain myself."

Stunned—she'd been ready to give up on the man *for now*—Moira wanted to make sure she understood what he was telling her. "Are you telling me that you're willing to partner up with me?"

He didn't answer her directly. "You said your lieutenant gave you forty-eight hours."

"Yes."

He shrugged. "I guess I can put up with anything for forty-eight hours—as long as that's the real time limit," he qualified, looking at her as if he could easily tell if she was lying.

She met his scrutiny head-on. "That's the real time limit he gave me."

He caught the last three words she'd added on and wondered if that was the loophole she was giving herself. Not that it really mattered. He'd been thinking about looking into the disturbed grave himself, just in his off-hours. What this woman proposed gave him official capacity to do it, which made the investigation that much easier to undertake.

Besides, she did have a point. Two sets of eyes—even devious ones as she appeared to have—were better than just one set.

And, whatever they found—or didn't find as the case might well be—this partnership was only for forty-eight hours.

"Okay, I'm in," he told her.

Since this man had turned out to be a human version of Mount Everest, her victory was almost heady. "That's great! There's only one more thing," she added as if in afterthought.

Davis was already beginning to regret his words. "What?" he asked her warily.

"What do I call you?" Moira asked. He still hadn't given her his name.

"As little as possible."

Compared to this man, Malloy was starting to seem like a veritable pussycat. "I still need to call you something."

He wasn't hung up on rank, labels or names. He shrugged indifferently. "Pick whatever you like."

Moira sighed. "Don't make this difficult—I have a sister working here who can make computers sit up and beg at will. If I give her a basic description of you, she can get me a name to pin to it in under an hour. It would be a waste of her time and the department's resources, but if that's the way you want to play it, then that's the way it'll have to be played."

Davis had a feeling she wasn't bluffing—which he found both irritating and somewhat intriguing at the same time. He supposed, in the absolute sense, he rather liked the fact that she was feisty as hell and didn't give up easily.

In a more practical sense, it would probably be the factor that would make him want to get his hands around her throat and squeeze—most likely in the not too distant future.

But, to forestall that eventuality for at least a little while, he decided to answer her question. "It's Davis."

"Ah, progress." He didn't miss the touch of sarcasm in her voice. "As in first name, or last?" she asked.

Rather than specify, he just said his whole name. "Davis Gilroy."

Moira smiled at him and although he told himself that it didn't matter either way, the woman did have a rather warm, attractive smile.

"Pleased to meet you, Detective Davis Gilroy." She put out her hand again and this time, to avoid another potential clash, he shook it. "You'll be working with me as part of the Robbery Division," she informed him. "Until we find out otherwise, this case is going to be worked as a grave robbery."

He looked at her, surprised. "You're kidding."

Just how had she managed to talk her superior into that? As far as he knew, there hadn't been a single reported incident of a grave robbery in all of Aurora's history.

He had his doubts that this was what it was, but right now he had no other explanation for it, either.

"Frequently and with aplomb," she replied to his response. "But I'm afraid I'm not kidding this time, Gilroy."

It was a shame that he didn't have a seat belt to fasten, Davis caught himself thinking, because he had a very strong feeling he was in for a very bumpy ride.

Chapter 4

Davis assumed that since he'd agreed to this short-lived partnership, the woman who had waylaid him on the stairs would now step aside and allow him to pass.

But she remained right where she was, still blocking his way to the next floor.

"So who will I be talking to, Gilroy?" she asked.

She'd managed to catch him off guard—again—even though he did his best not to show it. "You mean right now?"

She noted the slight shift in his jaw muscles. Why had her question surprised him? "No time like the present. We don't exactly have the luxury of time on our side."

Moira realized that there were a lot of things about

this detective she *didn't* know. "What department are you with?"

"Major Crimes," Davis answered. "But I thought we already settled that part. I told you I'd talk to the captain about this."

At least, he had assumed that she'd agreed with him when he'd told her that he could talk to his captain about investigating the case. He was starting to think that assumption wasn't a wise course when it came to Moira Cavanaugh.

Moira waved away the detective's words. "I can sell this better than you can," she told him. "I got my lieutenant's okay to investigate and that wasn't the easiest thing to do. Since he said yes, I figure he'd want me to use whatever resources I needed in order to bring this case to a swift close."

Davis was starting to get an uneasy feeling about this. He wasn't a rules-and-regulations kind of man, but neither did he appreciate an all-out rebel, either. He liked operating under the radar whenever possible. That wasn't accomplished by pairing up with a rebel, no matter how short the duration of that coupling might be.

"And you see me as a resource?" he questioned.

"It's a hunch," she told the detective matter-of-factly. "The Cavanaughs are really big on hunches."

This was just for forty-eight hours, he reminded himself. How bad could things get in forty-eight hours? And, who knew, maybe working together they'd stumble across something important.

"Then I guess we'd better turn around," he told her. "Major Crimes is on the sixth floor."

Moira looked up the length of the stairwell. "That's three and a half flights up."

Davis managed to keep the unexpected note of amusement he felt out of his voice. "That a problem, Cavanaugh?"

He was challenging her. She would have much rather ridden the elevator, but if he expected her to back off then he would be sorely disappointed.

"No, it's not a problem. Lead the way," Moira told him.

Turning sharply on the stairs, he began to lead the way to the sixth floor and Major Crimes.

Moira was determined to keep up with him. After all, she ran every morning just to keep in shape. But there was something very different about running in more or less a straight line compared to quickly climbing up the stairs at a speed Detective Gilroy had deliberately assumed.

She had stamina, but he had the advantage of longer legs. Plus she had the feeling that Gilroy did this sort of thing on a regular basis. Did that mean he was too impatient to wait for the sluggish elevator?

Impatience was often seen as a flaw by many and it gave her hope that the man she'd elected to partner up with wasn't as much of a self-contained robot as he pretended to be.

Wanting to ask the detective a question, Moira saved her energy—and her breath—until they reached the sixth floor. Once out of the stairwell and into the corridor, she reinitiated the conversation, convinced that if she didn't, Gilroy would be more than happy to remain silent until he was forced to speak.

She glanced down at his hand before beginning. There was no wedding ring on his third finger, no jewelry at all. Granted that not every married man wore a wedding ring, but she had a feeling that in Gilroy's case it was because he had no reason to wear one. She highly doubted that any reasonable woman would have willingly resigned herself to a life dedicated to speaking as little as possible, like a Franciscan monk who'd taken a vow of silence.

Silence had never been her thing. Questions fairly burst out of her mouth on a regular basis. Now was no exception.

"What were you doing at the cemetery so early in the morning, anyway?" she asked, addressing her question to his back since he was still walking ahead of her.

Davis came to a dead stop.

She wasn't prepared for the detective to stop walking so abruptly and she couldn't prevent herself from slamming right up against his broad, hard back.

Davis swung around and glared at her. "I want to make something very clear, Cavanaugh." He all but growled at her.

Moira put up her hand to stop his flow of words for a second. "You might have to wait until the stars stop swirling around my head," she quipped.

If she meant the remark to loosen him up a little,

it didn't. Gilroy didn't crack a smile or even seem to hear her.

"I'll help you investigate whatever's going on at the cemetery, but I'm not going to continue being on the receiving end of your idea of Twenty Questions," he snapped.

"How about if we both play?" she suggested with a wide smile. "You answer my questions and I'll answer yours." It seemed only fair to her.

"I don't have any questions," he informed her tersely. The less he knew about her, the easier it would be to walk away when the forty-eight hours were finally up.

Moira stared at him. "You're serious?" she asked incredulously. Had she stumbled across the one man in the state who had absolutely no curiosity?

The detective's expression remained immobile. "Totally."

She just couldn't get herself to believe him. "You have no questions for me?"

"None," he replied flatly.

Moira shook her head in complete disbelief. He really *was* a robot.

"Then you'd be the first," she told him.

She glanced down the hall and saw the open door that had *Major Crimes* written across the opaque glass in black block letters. "This must be the place," she declared cheerfully. Moira braced herself inwardly. Time to beard the lion in his den. "What did you say your captain's name was?"

"I didn't."

Just when she assumed he was leaving it up to her to find out, Gilroy said, "Ryan. His name is Captain Ryan."

She nodded, taking the information in. Walking inside the squad room, she immediately noted that the layout was the same as it was on the third floor. And, like her lieutenant, the superior officer here had a small, glass-enclosed space—whimsically called an office—to call his own.

From the look of it, Captain Ryan was currently in, and he was on the phone.

"Give me ten minutes," she told Davis.

He gave her a skeptical look as she started to walk toward the other end of the room. "You don't want me in there with you?"

"I wouldn't dream of intruding on your space, Gilroy. Wait here," she told him, nodding at the squad room. "If I find myself needing you for backup, I'll wave at you," she told him just before she proceeded to quickly stride toward the captain's office.

Unlike Lieutenant Carver, the man who oversaw Major Crimes had his door open despite the fact that he was still on the phone.

It was like watching an accident waiting to happen, Davis thought, perched on the corner of his desk as he looked across the room and observed her.

He fully expected to hear Ryan's voice come booming across the office once the almost annoyingly perky blonde began to state her case to ask for him on loan for the surreal purpose of looking into a case of possible grave robbery.

But five, then ten minutes went by and the walls did not shake, nor did Ryan's door rattle.

Davis continued to watch his temporary partner in mounting fascination.

Twelve minutes after she entered Ryan's inner sanctum, she came out again, an even wider smile—if possible—on her lips.

"Well?" he asked her somewhat skeptically once she reached him.

"Well, you've got a very nice captain," she told him, a glint of mischief in her diamond-blue eyes. "Oh, and you're mine for the next forty-eight hours," she added as if that bit of information amounted to just an afterthought instead of the crux of her visit.

Mike Manetti, one of the oldest detectives in the Major Crimes squad—and some felt way overdue to embrace retirement—grinned broadly at him as he and his very temporary partner passed by his less than tidy desk.

"Lucky so-and-so," Manetti quipped, keeping his assessment clean because of the woman with the notoriously taciturn detective.

Moira smiled at the white-haired, older detective. "I doubt he thinks so," she said as if confiding in Manetti.

"Then Gilroy's a slower learner than I gave him credit for," Manetti told her with a pronounced wink. "Make the most of this, boy. Make the most of this," Manetti advised, raising his voice so that it followed both of them out into the hall.

Davis deliberately ignored what Manetti had just

said. Instead, he thought of his captain and the cheerful expression on the other man's face.

"What the hell did you say to Ryan?" Davis asked.

He'd been fairly convinced that the captain, in the final analysis, would turn down her request, which would have admittedly put him back to square one, investigating whatever was going on at the cemetery alone. All in all, that was not exactly an unwelcome scenario even though he had already admitted to her that two heads were usually better than one.

"That my lieutenant would appreciate his cooperation in lending out one of his best detectives for this rather unique and hush-hush investigation into some unorthodox dealings at St. Joseph's Cemetery. I mentioned that some of Aurora's most prominent citizens had loved ones who were buried there and that they wanted this looked into and taken care of quickly and quietly." And then that damnable grin of hers returned to momentarily sidetrack his attention. "Oh, and I might have also mentioned that my great-uncle sent his best."

Davis looked at her suspiciously. Here it was; the crux of it. "Great-uncle?"

Moira didn't even try to suppress the smile that spread across her face. "Yes. Brian Cavanaugh. He's the Chief of—"

"Ds, yes, I know," he all but snapped, saving her the trouble of making what he assumed was an announcement. His suspicions heightened. "I thought that you Cavanaughs made this big deal about climbing up through the ranks strictly on your own merits without relying on the Cavanaugh name or connections."

"We do," she informed him openly and surprisingly artlessly.

She was totally blowing his mind. Didn't she hear the contradiction?

"Then what was *that* all about?" he asked, nodding back in the general direction of his captain's office.

"That was using leverage to get *you* on the case. I'm already on it, remember?" she replied innocently.

"Okay." He didn't really accept that, but for now, he let it drop. "And what makes you think I'm one of Ryan's 'best' detectives?" he asked, using the same term she had used earlier. Did she think she was endearing herself with this baseless flattery?

"You'd have to be," she pointed out without an iota of guile. "With that wounded-bear attitude of yours, if you weren't one of his best, you would have gotten yourself tossed out on your ear a long time ago." She flashed a quick, spasmodic smile at him, adding, "That's called deductive reasoning."

His eyes narrowed as he glared at her. "That's called hot air," Davis pointed out.

"Po*ta*to, po*ta*to," she countered. "By the way," she told him, completely devoid of fanfare or ego, "I'm primary on this." It was best to lay down the ground rules right from the start.

Moira fully expected the detective to balk at that and was surprised when he merely shrugged.

"Figured you would be," he commented.

Moira congratulated herself on containing her surprise. "Oh, and why's that?"

"You brought the case to me, not the other way around."

"I've got a hunch you don't bring anything to anybody," she couldn't help saying. The man definitely wasn't one of those kids whose report card read, "Works and plays well with others."

Still, she had to admit that he intrigued her. Maybe even more than just a little.

Gilroy studied her for a prolonged moment and she had absolutely no idea what was going on in the detective's head. She really hoped that this wasn't going to be a regular thing while they worked together. Moira hated being in the dark about *anything*, especially when it came to her partner. Warner wasn't a bundle of joy, but he was very predictable and that, in turn, made her feel confident.

"Maybe we will work together well, after all," he exhorted.

That could have knocked her over with a feather. It was official. Detective Davis Gilroy was entirely unpredictable.

Clearing her throat, Moira moved on.

"Okay, first order of business, we take the elevator down. I get enough exercise first thing every morning jogging around this city for an hour."

"Every morning?" he questioned, making it sound as if he found her claim suspect.

"That's what I said."

"Why?"

She gave him the same answer she gave herself every morning. "It wakes me up."

"Getting out of bed should be able to do that for you," he said drily.

"You'd think so, wouldn't you?" she quipped, her remark indicating that it clearly didn't.

With that, she led the way to the far end of the hall where the elevator was located. She pressed for it, hoping that it would show up before Gilroy decided to take the stairs again. She wasn't altogether certain the man would wait for her by the precinct's rear doors if he got there first.

Though she had been the one to talk him into joining forces with her, she had no idea what to expect from this tall, handsome walking clam.

The next moment she made a mental note to ask Valri to look into his background and give her a thumbnail sketch. Maybe if she had that, she'd be a little more prepared when it came to what to expect from him.

She had a very strong feeling that even after they spent some time on the job together, Gilroy wasn't the type to fill in the blanks unless he was absolutely forced to. And while she did like her share of surprises, she also liked to know what she was getting herself into.

Her instincts told her that Gilroy was a good cop and a damn fine detective—what she'd told him about her reasoning was true—but that still didn't tell her enough about Gilroy the man, other than that he was an only child—and that was something she'd uncovered on her own. Most of all, she wanted to know how far she could trust him, and if he had her back.

"You want to drive?" she asked him as they got into the elevator.

He looked at her before answering.

She was beginning to think that carefully analyzing the person he was talking to was a thing with him and that he never spoke just off the cuff.

"You don't?" he asked her after a beat.

Moira shrugged. "I don't care one way or the other. Why?"

"I just figured that, as primary, you'd want to be in control."

His reasoning was just a tad flawed. Odd as it might have seemed, that gave her a little bit of hope again. She wasn't after perfect when it came to a partner, she was after sharp.

"Driving a car doesn't make me in control. Staying in control of the situation makes me in control," she told him matter-of-factly. "That doesn't include insisting on playing a glorified taxi driver."

Her response had him regarding her thoughtfully for another long moment before conceding, "Okay, I'll drive."

She had a hunch that he preferred it that way. *Score, Cavanaugh side.*

Contrary to the ending in *Casablanca*, Moira thought, this did *not* have the earmarks of the beginning of a long, beautiful friendship.

But she would give it her best shot—at least for now.

She was a firm believer in working with the present. That way, if all went well, the future would take care of itself.

Chapter 5

"I'm assuming that you want to use your car," Davis said, waiting for her to point the vehicle out in the parking lot.

"Why would you assume that?" Moira asked. "We'll use yours. After all, you're used to the way your car handles and you're the one who's driving."

Davis had to admit her reasoning made sense. "Logical."

"You sound surprised," she noted.

He raised and lowered his shoulders in a vague, disinterested shrug. "Maybe I am," Davis allowed, leading the way to his vehicle.

"Okay, partner," she said, getting into his car, "our first stop is going to be the cemetery."

Gilroy had just turned the key in the ignition, but

the car remained in Park. "Don't call me that," he retorted angrily. "You are *not* my partner."

"Don't be shy, Gilroy," she said to him. "Tell me what you *really* think."

His flash of temper had taken even him by surprise. He worked now to get it under control. "I *think* you should call me by my name or just detective."

Moira stared at the man in the driver's seat, wondering just what the hell had happened here. "But not 'partner.'"

One look at his face and she could see that there was no way to penetrate the barrier he'd just thrown up. "Not partner," he echoed.

And they said women were difficult to deal with, Moira thought sarcastically.

But she'd gone out of her way to ask for him. Rescinding her request so early into the game was out of the question. She was stuck—at least for the next forty-seven and a half hours.

"Mind if I ask why?" she asked.

"Yes—" he bit the word off "—I do mind."

Okay, there was just so much patience she had available. This was going to get resolved—one way or another.

"Well, too bad," she retorted. "I'm primary and if you're going to bite my head off, I'm going to need to know why."

What he wanted to say was that it was none of her business—but maybe, in a way, it was. So he grudgingly dispensed a few words. "Because I refuse to have anyone else on my conscience."

Moira shook her head. "Still need more of an explanation than that," she informed him. "And put the car into Drive—I'm assuming you can drive and talk at the same time," she interjected, "because right now, we're wasting time."

Scowling, Davis did as she'd asked, at least as far as the vehicle was concerned. Backing out of the space he was in, the detective shifted the transmission into Drive and left the precinct's rear parking lot.

"Okay, you're driving," she noted after several minutes of silence had gone by, "but that's only half of what I asked you to do. Talk to me, Gilroy—notice how I used your name there and didn't make a reference to what most will assume is our on-the-job relationship? Why did you just jump down my throat when I called you my p—"

Unwilling to hear the term, Davis cut her off. "Because the last two people who called themselves that are in the same cemetery we're driving to right now."

"So you lost your part—" she began and again she got no further.

"I lost *two*," Davis emphasized. "Two of them in three years."

"Unfortunate," she allowed, "as well as unusual. But it happens. More than a lot of us like to think about, but that still doesn't mean—"

"It means that I *don't want* another partner. I only agreed to go along with this because it's got a preset time limit. As far as I'm concerned, we're just two detectives from two entirely different departments, riding in a car together and trying to get a few answers about a possible case."

He wasn't about to be preached to by a so-called golden girl from a family who, for the most part, led charmed lives.

"Did each of them take a bullet for you?" Moira asked.

Pulling over to the curb, Davis abruptly stopped the car. "No," he retorted. "Anything else?"

Yes, there was something else, she thought. She wanted to know why he was being so mysterious about it. Everyone had wounds, some large, some small, but no one in this line of work came out the other end untouched.

"If they didn't take a bullet for you, why are you being so hard on yourself?" she asked.

"*Because* they took a bullet," he snapped. It was obvious that he thought she was being obtuse.

"And you're...what? Some superhero who's supposed to deflect bullets from hitting your partner?"

Disgusted, Davis turned off the engine. "This isn't going to work."

"No, it's not," she agreed. But instead of telling him to turn around and go back to the precinct—the way he fully expected her to—Moira said, "Not until you get rid of that massive chip on your shoulder and stop snapping at every second word I say."

He glared at her. She was really getting on his nerves. "Maybe you talk too much."

Her shrug was indifferent. "I've been told that.

But you obviously don't talk enough," she countered pointedly.

"You just said I jumped down your throat."

"Talk." She emphasized the word again. "Not snap." Then, before he could stop her, Moira leaned over and pulled the key out of the ignition. To his amazement, she hid it behind her back. "Now we're not going anywhere until you tell me what else is bothering you."

His look only grew darker. Anyone else might have relented—or at least cringed. Moira stubbornly held her ground.

"Other than you?" he retorted.

Moira inclined her head. "Other than me."

He'd had just about enough of this back-and-forth jousting. "We're supposed to be solving a possible case," he reminded her tersely. "Not having a road-side therapy session."

Instead of backing down the way he hoped, she flashed an annoying smile at him.

"Two for the price of one, Gilroy—no charge for the therapy session," she added glibly. "Now, what's this thing you have against having a partner? You don't strike me as someone who's superstitious," she told him.

It wasn't superstition if you kept getting proved right time after time—beginning with his parents. He'd survived the accident, they hadn't. Likewise with his partners—they'd either gotten pinned down or ambushed. Each time it was the same. He'd survived. They hadn't. He wasn't about to go through this again.

"And maybe you're not as good at reading people

as you think," he told her, about to open the door on his side.

"Where are you going?" Moira demanded.

He didn't have to tell her but he did. "Back to the precinct. We're not that far away from it. I can walk from here."

He started to swing open the door on his side when she leaned over and grabbed him by the arm. Because she'd caught him by surprise, she managed to get him to sink down in his seat again.

"And tell your captain what?" she asked.

"That you couldn't put up with me and decided you'd made a mistake. I won't have any trouble convincing him," he assured her tersely. "Now, are you going to let go of my wrist or are you waiting for me to gnaw it off?"

A hint of a smile curved the corners of her mouth. "Might be interesting to watch at that," she allowed. Then, growing serious, she said, "Here," and returned his key to him.

Davis looked down at it in his hand. "You want me to drive back to the precinct?" he grumbled. Maybe she was feeling guilty for putting him through the wringer. He didn't care about the reason; he just wanted this to be over.

"No," Moira countered patiently, enunciating each word, "I want you to drive to the cemetery. The gravesite we're investigating isn't in the precinct, it's in the cemetery."

Davis regarded the key he was holding thoughtfully, then finally put it into the ignition and turned it.

The engine came back to life. Grudgingly, he began to drive the vehicle without sparing her a glance. "You don't give up easily, do you?"

"See, you're learning about me already," Moira remarked far too cheerfully to suit his mood.

"We're not going to be together long enough to learn things about each other." His voice was dark and foreboding.

She merely smiled at him in response. "We'll see," she told him.

They might not even last the entire forty-eight hours, Davis couldn't help thinking. Not if he gave in to this growing urge he had to strangle her.

Moira's second, far more intense look around the area where she'd first noticed that the gravesite had been disturbed convinced her that her hunch was right. Gilroy had obviously stumbled across something going on at the cemetery.

From the looks of the immediate area directly in front of the headstone, the ground had been disturbed, quite possibly dug up, very recently.

She squatted for an even closer look and was surprised when Gilroy followed suit, squatting directly beside her.

When she looked at him quizzically, he said, "Two sets of eyes, remember?"

She nodded then asked the next logical question. "And what do your eyes see?"

"Same as yours," he answered. "The dirt in front of the headstone's been freshly packed."

Well, at least they were on the same page about that, she thought.

"Yet there's been no addition to the headstone," she observed. "That means that no spouse or relative is now eternally resting beside our original occupant, Mrs. Emily Jenkins," she said, glancing at the name she'd noted earlier. "So why the disturbance?" she asked, looking thoughtfully at the ground in front of the headstone.

"Somebody obviously dug her up," Gilroy said, a touch of impatience in his voice.

Maybe not the woman herself, but at least the coffin, she thought. Out loud she allowed, "Maybe. But if so, why?"

"Only one way to find out," Davis answered, pointing out the obvious.

"Can I help you?"

The unexpected question came from directly behind them.

Startled, Moira swung around and found herself looking at a somewhat rumpled, sleepy-eyed man in tan, grass-stained jeans and a work shirt. The man, most likely the groundskeeper, Moira guessed, was round-shouldered, looked to be around forty-plus and did not appear to be holding up all that well.

He was also scowling.

"Detectives Cavanaugh and Gilroy," Moira said officially, identifying herself and the man beside her before venturing to even begin to answer the groundskeeper's question. First she had a question of her own. "And you are…?"

"Asking you if I can help you," the man replied, repeating his question.

"You could start with your name," Moira responded. She followed her request with a ghost of a smile that she didn't mean.

The man's deep-set eyes grew even smaller as he regarded her closely. "Why do you want to know my name?" he asked.

"He's as helpful as you are," Moira murmured to the detective beside her. Out of the corner of her eye, she caught a glimmer of Gilroy's frown. "Because we're investigating a possible crime committed here," she told the groundskeeper.

"There's been no crime," the man informed them indignantly, looking from one detective to the other. "I would have known."

Because you're so sharp and on top of things, Moira thought.

"The ground around the grave's been disturbed," Davis pointed out, annoyance framing every syllable. Unlike Moira, he had no patience and no time to waste with niceties.

But at least he speaks!

It was all Moira could do to keep the words from leaping from her lips. She gave Davis an approving look that only seemed to intensify his scowl.

"Sometimes animals dig around here," the groundskeeper told them, shifting his weight from one foot to the other.

"Not the full length and width of a grave," Moira

countered. "If we dig up the grave, what'll we find?" she asked the older man pointedly.

"A lawsuit slapped on the police department by the man's family as well as the cemetery unless you have a court order." He looked from one detective to the other, this time with a trace of superiority evident. "You don't have a court order with you, do you?" the groundskeeper assumed smugly.

The way he asked, it was obvious that he expected a negative response to his question.

Rather than say anything to the man, Moira took out her cell phone and began snapping photographs of the gravesite from all angles. Because he stood as immobile as one of the marble statues, she moved the groundskeeper out of the way then proceeded to take a full panoramic view of the grave in question.

"We'll be back," she promised. "And if that grave looks any different than the way it does on these pictures, you're going to have a great deal of explaining to do," she promised him. With that, she turned on her heel and addressed her reluctant partner. "Let's go, Gilroy."

Davis fell into place beside her as they walked away from the grave and the groundskeeper.

"He's not as dull-witted as he looks," Davis commented.

Something else they agreed on, she thought in surprise. "I'd say not by a long shot."

"He could just be protective of his job," Davis suggested, speculating. It was obvious he thought the odds of that were rather slim.

"Maybe," she agreed slowly, thinking. "Or maybe there's more."

"Maybe," he agreed. "The shame of it is that we're probably not going to find out."

She looked at him in surprise. "Why would you say that?"

"Because we need a court order to dig up whatever's in that grave." Had she forgotten about that?

Reaching the car, she waited for him to release the locks to open the door on her side, but even when he did, she remained standing outside the vehicle.

"I got that part," Moira commented.

"Did you also figure out how we're going to get a court order without any tangible evidence to show any self-respecting judge? There's no way he or she would rule in our favor."

When she merely smiled broadly at him, he told himself not to rise to the bait. He wasn't going to ask her just what she had up her sleeve. It was obvious to him that she wouldn't be looking so pleased with herself if she didn't have something tucked up there.

His resolve lasted just long enough to open the door on his side and get in behind the steering wheel.

At that point he finally gave in to the curiosity suddenly and relentlessly nibbling away at him. "What?" he finally asked impatiently.

Moira played the moment out a little longer, just until she'd gotten into the passenger side of the car and buckled up her seat belt.

Then, as Gilroy started up the vehicle, she said to him, "The beauty of being a Cavanaugh is that there's always someone in the family to turn to no matter what the situation you're facing calls for. Since you've made a religion of keeping to yourself, you're probably not aware of the fact that the Cavanaugh family tree has at least two judges in it."

"At least?" he echoed. "Don't you know how many?" He assumed she was an expert when it came to flaunting all the various so-called branches of her family tree.

Moira nodded, admitting, "There might be more, but I have to admit that I'm still in the process of learning everyone's name, the nature of their relationship to everyone else and what they all do within the department—or how they're affiliated with it if they're not working directly within the police force. For instance, one of my second cousins is a vet," she told him, referring to Patience Cavanaugh Coltrane.

"So what all those words that just came flooding out of your mouth mean is that we're getting our court order, right?"

Moira's eyes, he noted unwillingly, seemed to sparkle like gleeful stars as she happily answered, "You bet we are."

Chapter 6

Judge Blake Kincannon rose from behind his desk the moment he heard the knock on his chamber door. He'd been waiting for them.

"Door's not locked. Come in, Moira," he said, welcoming the young woman he had spoken to on the phone less than fifteen minutes ago.

She wasn't alone, as Blake already knew she wouldn't be.

He regarded the tall, serious-looking detective who entered in her wake, smiling at both of them with equal warmth.

She'd gotten through to the judge faster than even she had anticipated. There were definite advantages to being connected to a support system as all-encompassing and large as the Cavanaugh family.

"Thank you for seeing us on such short notice, Judge," Moira said as she walked into the man's fourth-floor chambers.

"We're family, Moira. Outside of the courtroom, you can call me Blake," Greer's husband told her. He turned to look at Davis. "And this is your partner?"

Moira didn't want to correct the Judge, especially since he was about to do them a huge favor. But she didn't want Gilroy getting upset again, either.

She chose middle ground.

"This is the detective I'm working on the case with," Moira responded, nudging the conversation along in a slightly different direction. "Davis Gilroy from Major Crimes. Gilroy, this is Judge Blake Kincannon."

"Otherwise known as Greer's husband," Blake told him wryly as he shook the other detective's hand. "Sorry," Blake apologized, "I just assumed you were partners."

"Just until we figure out what's going on at the local cemetery," Moira explained before the other detective could say anything.

Blake nodded, accepting the explanation. "Why don't you sit down and tell me what you need for that to happen?" Blake suggested, gesturing toward the two seats in front of his desk.

"As I told you on the phone, we need a court order to exhume a coffin from St. Joseph's Cemetery." She repeated the reason she'd given him when she'd called. "The ground under and in front of the headstone has been disturbed recently and we'd like to see if anything was either taken from or added to the gravesite." Her words echoed back to her and she gave him an apologetic smile. "I know it seems kind of strange—"

Blake raised his hand, stopping her apology. "Don't worry about it. The longer I'm in this job, the less anything surprises me. Do you have any kind of evidence to back up your—I'm assuming hunch?" he finally said.

"I—we—" Moira corrected herself since she had, after all, brought Gilroy into the judge's chambers with her "—have pictures of the area in question." She took out her cell phone.

Pressing the app for photographs, she quickly pulled up the pictures she'd taken earlier at the cemetery. Turning the phone over to Blake, she slid to the edge of her seat as she watched him go through the array.

The judge looked over the evidence carefully then raised his eyes to glance at Greer's cousin. "And you took these…?"

"Just before I called you," Moira told him.

"Certainly looks as if the grave has been tampered with." Blake turned the cell phone back to her. "I'd say this is definitely worth looking into. Give me a minute," he requested.

Pulling up a screen on his computer monitor, he skimmed through a menu until he found the form he needed to sign and turn over to Moira. He hit Print and then leaned back to the small table where his legal aide had set up a new printer just a week ago. Two seconds later, he was holding the appropriate form in his hand.

"Tell me," Blake said as he placed his signature on

the required line and then nodded toward the silent detective beside Moira, "does he ever talk?"

"Only when he feels he needs to," Moira replied, doing her best to look serious.

Blake handed the form to Moira and turned his attention to the detective who had come in with her.

"Let me give you a friendly little piece of advice, Detective. Speak up. Cavanaugh women rarely come up for air and if you don't speak up once in a while, you'll find yourself just swept up in their wake. I speak from experience," he told Davis with a warm laugh.

Since their business was in essence concluded, Davis rose to his feet. The judge followed suit. Davis noticed that the man had maybe on inch on him, if that. "I'll keep that in mind, Judge."

"Just something to think about," Blake told him. He walked the duo to the door. "See you at the next family gathering," he said to Moira. "You, too," he added, looking at Davis. "Andrew Cavanaugh's known for throwing parties for no other reason than because it's Saturday, or February, or the sun is shining—and his credo has always been the more, the merrier."

"Thank you for this," Moira said quickly, indicating the court order. She didn't want to give Gilroy a chance to say anything to the judge about Andrew's parties. There was time enough for her to raise that topic later. Right now, she didn't want to give Gilroy another reason to be disgruntled.

Blake nodded. "Be sure to let me know how it turns out."

"Count on it," Moira promised as she left the judge's chambers.

Blake paused to shake Davis's hand before the detective left. "Remember," Blake reminded him, "speak up."

"He meant that, you know," she told Davis as they walked down the hall to the elevator.

"What?" Davis reached past her and pressed the down button. The elevator arrived almost immediately. "To speak up?"

"That, too, probably," she conceded. "But I'm talking about Uncle Andrew's philosophy." Stepping into the elevator car, she waited until he got on next to her and then pressed for the first floor. Her arm brushed against him as she did so. The warm shiver ambushed her out of nowhere. On a whim, she decided to see how Gilroy would react to the judge's suggestion if she pushed it a little. "You're invited to the next family gathering—especially since we're working together."

"By the time the next 'family gathering' happens," Davis told her, "we won't be." And that would be a good thing, he thought, because this woman was really getting to him—in a way he just couldn't allow. "And, besides, I'm not family, anyway."

No one else got on and the elevator went straight down to the first floor. "You're a cop. That automatically makes you family as far as Uncle Andrew is concerned."

"Why?" Davis asked. It didn't make any sense to him.

Arriving on the ground floor, they got out. "Uncle

Andrew used to be the chief of police until he took early retirement."

Davis laughed shortly. "Couldn't take the pressure anymore?"

Maybe in his world, people did that, she thought, feeling suddenly protective of the granduncle she hadn't always realized she was related to. "His wife went missing and he had five kids to raise," she corrected tersely.

Despite his resolution to steer clear of personal topics, he found that Cavanaugh had managed—once again—to arouse his curiosity. "She walked out on him?"

Moira enjoyed correcting him. "No. As it turned out, she was in a car accident—went over the side of the road and into the lake," she summarized quickly. "And when she came to, she'd lost her memory."

Yeah, right, Davis thought. He'd learned to hold stories like that highly suspect. "Convenient," he murmured.

Moira did her best not to lose her temper as they descended the front steps toward the parking lot. "Not really—and she really did lose her memory. They found the car and everyone figured she was dead even though they couldn't find a body. But in between taking care of his family, Uncle Andrew never gave up hope that his wife was alive. He pieced together and followed up on every single clue he could find."

"And?" Davis asked with a touch of impatience when she didn't continue.

Moira suppressed a smile, pleased that she had managed to get him sufficiently interested enough to ask her the question.

"And eventually he found her. She was a waitress at this little diner up the coast. He confronted her with family photographs and stories and convinced her to come back with him, hoping to jog her memory."

The women he knew would have thought the man to be a stalker and would head in the opposite direction. But he asked, "Did he?"

This time she did smile. "Eventually, yes."

He laughed drily again. "I was right. You Cavanaughs are a stubborn bunch."

Moira's grin was wide and self-satisfied. "You don't know the half of it."

"You're right, and I'm not going to know," he informed her. Glancing at his watch, he announced, "Less than forty-four hours to go."

Rather than get annoyed that he was keeping such close track of the time, Moira said brightly, "Just think, if this job doesn't work out for you, you can get one as the town crier."

He ignored the comment. Instead, reaching his car, he released the locks and got in behind the wheel again. "Back to the cemetery?"

Moira nodded. "Back to the cemetery," she confirmed.

Avery Weaver, the groundskeeper, frowned as he looked up from raking a small patch of leaves that had fallen from a large, shady deciduous tree.

"You again?" he fairly snarled, seeing the two detectives walking into the cemetery.

"Looks that way," Moira replied. "We've got that court order you were so anxious to look at." She took it out of her pocket and handed it over to the scraggly man. "And we brought friends," she added, indicating the navy van pulling up behind Gilroy's car.

Written in large block letters on the side of the van were the words Crime Scene Investigations. Stopping directly behind Davis's unmarked car, the van's driver and passenger both disembarked.

Two members of Sean Cavanaugh's CSI team looked to Moira for their directions. "Which grave is it, Moira?" the driver asked.

"It's that one," Davis told him before Moira had a chance, pointing out the grave in question.

Moira looked in her nonpartner's direction. "I see you're taking Blake's advice and speaking up."

Davis shrugged carelessly. "The man sounded like he knew what he was talking about," was all he said as he turned to watch the two CSI agents mark off the grave and then begin digging.

He wasn't the only one watching. But, unlike Davis, in the groundskeeper's case, Weaver was looking on uneasily.

And then Weaver turned toward them. "You need me for anything else?" he asked, addressing his question to Moira.

"Not unless you know of another grave around here that's been disturbed or tampered with," Moira told him.

The tall, lanky man pulled back his thin shoulders, emphasizing his complete lack of physique.

"No, but there's going to be a burial at the other end of the cemetery in about an hour and I should get over there to make sure everything's ready for it."

Moira inclined her head. She saw no reason to have the man hang around right now, getting in their way. For the time being, his usefulness had ended.

"Where can we find you in case we have any more questions?" she asked.

"I've got a room right off the office." Weaver pointed in the general direction of the small one-story building. And then he added in a vague manner, "I'll be around."

"Sure he will," Davis commented under his breath as the groundskeeper scurried away.

Moira glanced in his direction. "You don't trust him, either?"

"The man's a weasel," Davis observed. "What's to trust?"

Moira laughed. "Well, at least we're on the same page when it comes to that," she commented.

Ninety minutes later, Emily Jenkins's coffin was exhumed and brought up out of what was to have obviously been the woman's final resting place.

The two crime scene investigators who had just hoisted the coffin placed it on the ground next to the large hole they had excavated.

Riley O'Shea looked toward Moira, aware that she was the primary on the case. "You want to do the honors?" he asked.

Moira shook her head. The last thing she wanted to do was to pry the lid from the coffin and find herself looking down at a twenty-year-old corpse. "You're the experts here."

"Okay, brace yourself, Detectives. This is not going to smell pretty," Riley warned, adding, "If you've got handkerchiefs with you, I'd suggest using them."

Moira shook her head. "Never carry one," she said just before she felt a handkerchief being put into her hand. Surprised, she looked to her left and saw that Gilroy was giving her the one he'd taken out of his pocket.

"Don't you want it?" she asked him.

Davis's expression remained solemn as he shook his head. "I wouldn't be giving it to you if I did, would I?" he asked her tersely.

The man was a total puzzle to her. "Thanks," she murmured just as Riley and Conrad, the other CSI agent, succeeded in prying open the coffin lid.

The stench that first greeted them was overwhelming and, for a moment, Moira thought the coffee and bag of corn chips she'd consumed in lieu of breakfast this morning was going to be coming up.

Mind over matter, Moi. Mind over matter, she counseled herself, thinking the words over and over again like a mantra until she finally regained control over her cramping stomach muscles.

"What were you hoping to find?" Riley asked them, setting the lid to the side.

"A reason why the grave was disturbed," Davis replied.

Out of the corner of his eye he saw Cavanaugh nod her head, agreeing with his response. He noted that the color had drained ever so slightly from her face. He wondered if she was the type to faint and so positioned himself closer to her, just in case he had to move quickly to catch her.

"You okay?" he asked.

"I'm fine," she answered a little too quickly and a little too tersely, even to her own ear. "Thanks," she added, her voice a little more subdued.

Riley examined the coffin's contents more closely. And then he shook his head, indicating that he didn't find anything amiss.

"My guess is some kids playing a prank, or maybe this was a frat initiation that didn't quite gel. In any case, nothing seems to be missing. Body's in the coffin," the man reported. "You want us to take it to the lab, or just put it back?" he asked her. "Your call."

Moira had just gotten herself to look into the coffin. Wearing plastic gloves, she started to conduct her own review of the coffin's interior when she heard the groundskeeper shout.

"Put it back!" Weaver ordered, walking toward the emptied gravesite.

The groundskeeper was getting on her nerves. Moira turned to look at the gaunt man. "I thought you had a burial to prepare for."

"I do—just as soon as I get you people the hell off the cemetery's property." Now that nothing had apparently been found to be amiss, he had grown bolder in his attitude. "You got what you came for. You opened up that poor woman's grave and disturbed her eternal rest. Now put her coffin back in, fill up her grave and leave," he ordered. "Or this time, I *will* start legal proceedings against the police department—and you two in particular," he snarled, glaring at both of them.

"It is just me, or did his grammar just get better?" Moira asked her faux partner.

Davis would have preferred to not take a side but, given the choice, he picked hers. Especially since she was right and the groundskeeper had gotten on his nerves right from the start.

"Definitely better," Davis agreed.

"I've got the cemetery's lawyer on speed dial," Weaver announced, taking out his cell phone and holding it aloft as if it were some sort of detonation device he intended to use.

"Good for you," Davis said in a low, even voice that was definitely not friendly. "Now put that damn thing away before someone makes you swallow it."

Weaver grew paler than he already was and took a shaky step back from the tall detective he was obviously afraid of.

"You can't threaten me like that," Weaver cried angrily.

"He didn't," Moira pointed out. "Detective Gilroy said 'someone,' he didn't specify who. Did you hear him specify who?" she asked, turning toward first Riley then Conrad.

"Not us," Riley denied for both of them as they worked carefully to lower the coffin into the grave without damaging it. "Didn't hear him say a name. No. How about you, Conrad?"

The more heavyset man shook his head. "Nope," he answered.

"Just put everything back the way you found it— and that means every shovelful of dirt!" Weaver instructed before he walked angrily away.

"Well, *that* went well," Moira muttered under her breath.

Davis was looking down at the coffin that was being reburied.

"Yeah," he agreed, more to himself than with her. He sounded even less happy about the outcome than the woman he'd been thrown together with.

Chapter 7

Detective Davis Gilroy was a man who liked silence more than most people did. The absence of noise allowed him to clear his mind and to think more clearly. Occasionally he might put on the radio as he was driving, but for the most part, silence suited his purposes quite well.

But as he drove them back to the precinct, the silence inside his car struck him as unnatural. Not because of the silence itself but because there was silence in his car while Moira Cavanaugh was in it.

As each minute passed the effect of this silence only grew *more* discomforting.

Finally, unable to endure the tortured absence of sound any longer, Davis glanced at the other occupant in his vehicle as he slowed at a red light.

"So now what?"

Moira leaned back against her seat and sighed. "Now I take this back to Carver and try to convince him to let me keep working on it. Technically, I still have more than twenty-four hours left."

"Work on *what*?" Davis asked. "That was the only grave that was disturbed and it looks like whoever disturbed it did so just for the hell of it."

Frustrated, Moira shrugged. Gilroy wasn't helping, she thought. But she couldn't deny that he was just asking questions that she knew Carver would ask. She needed an answer for the lieutenant, but what?

"I don't know," she responded, irritated. She couldn't shake the feeling that they were missing something. "Stake the place out. Wait for something else suspicious to happen."

The expression on Gilroy's face told her he thought she was really reaching now.

"I don't know about your department," he told her, "but mine doesn't exactly go around begging for work. We've got enough cases to keep all the people who work there busy."

Moira sighed. Much as she hated to admit it, he had a point. One she didn't know how to discount, especially since she knew Carver would say the same thing. "Mine, too."

If she believed that, then what was the problem? "So what makes you think your boss—or mine—is going to sign off on more time devoted to this wild-goose chase?"

Moira sighed again. He was right, and yet she just

couldn't let go of it. "Because at times, I still believe in Santa Claus—or want to at any rate."

There was something akin to pity as well as exasperation in Gilroy's eyes as he told her, "You just go on believing, Cavanaugh. Me, the second your lieutenant says, 'Case closed,' I'm back in Major Crimes."

She knew he meant it. "Give me a chance to talk Carver into it," Moira requested. "You never know, just maybe when…"

But Davis had never been one to build castles in the sky. Not since just before he turned thirteen. "From what I hear about the man, I think the phrase you might be looking for is 'when pigs fly.'"

She looked at Gilroy, wondering what he'd been like as a child. Had he been born with that dour look on his face? "You never believed in Santa Claus at all, did you?"

His expression never changed. He was not about to get pulled into a frivolous conversation. "Nope."

No surprise there—just sadness. "I kind of figured that," she told him. "What you need, Gilroy, is magic in your life."

"What I need, Cavanaugh," he countered, "is to get back to working cases on my own. Solo," he emphasized for good measure in case she missed his point.

"Don't you ever get lonely?" she asked, momentarily forgetting her disappointment about the would-be case and turning her attention to the man driving to the precinct. Coming from the background she did, where six siblings wasn't even considered a crowd, she found herself not just feeling sorry for Gilroy but feeling a growing urge to *fix* him.

"I make it a point to never get lonely," Davis answered. "There're fewer complications that way." His tone underscored his point.

Okay, maybe she needed a more direct approach here.

"Look," she began, "why don't you come to Uncle Andrew's next—"

"No," he told her firmly. He didn't have to hear her out. He could tell from her tone where she was going with this.

Moira knew that Andrew wouldn't mind. He loved his family, cooking and bringing wounded people around, the latter not necessarily referring to physical wounds. Besides, Blake had already mentioned the subject to him when he'd issued the exhumation order.

Determined, Moira tried again. "You'll—"

"No," Davis repeated more forcefully.

The man was nothing short of infuriating, she thought, trying a third time. "But—"

"No!"

So much for the polite approach. "Are you trying to set some sort of record for how many times you can say no before we reach the precinct, Gilroy?"

"If I have to," he allowed. "But I'm kind of counting on you being a faster learner than that."

Moira bit her tongue and retreated.

She told herself that there was a difference between retreating and giving up. Besides, right now, she needed to use whatever mental resources she had to try to convince her lieutenant that there was something going on at the cemetery and she just needed a little more time to uncover what that was.

She had no proof to offer him, only a hunch that was currently eating away at her gut—and growing bigger by the moment.

"Have it your way," she told him, lapsing back into silence.

Davis had a strong feeling this wasn't the last he was going to hear of it, no matter what Cavanaugh pretended to the contrary.

Arriving at the robbery squad room a short while later, Moira saw that the lieutenant was in and that his door was closed, as usual.

She glanced at the detective who had returned to her squad room with her. "You want to come in with me?" she asked Gilroy.

He stopped at her desk. "I think I'll sit this one out," he answered. "I'm pretty good at reading expressions and body language. I'll figure out what's going on," he assured her.

It was just as well, Moira supposed. She didn't have a good feeling about this and she didn't exactly welcome the idea of having someone watch her fall flat on her face. Carver wasn't much for going outside the lines and taking a chance on something, so his response to her entreaty was all but a foregone conclusion.

Still, she had to try.

"Find something already?" Carver asked after he'd

responded to her knock and told her to come in and shut the door behind her.

"Actually, nothing seemed to be missing from the coffin." Each word she uttered tasted almost bitter in her mouth.

Carver's deep-set eyes became almost large as he glared at her, her words obviously replaying themselves in his head.

"You dug up the coffin?" he cried, startled. "You got permission from the deceased's family to dig it up?"

"No. Not that we didn't try," she interjected. "But there was no family that we could find."

Several shades of red took turns washing over the lieutenant's face. "What!"

"I had a court order," she told him quickly, aware that the first thing Carver would jump on was that the department could very well be sued. That part, Moira gleaned from the fact that the parade of colors had not yet receded from the man's face.

"And you still found nothing," Carver concluded angrily.

"That I could see," Moira qualified, ready to launch into myriad reasons why there still might be something to the case, something that hadn't been immediately apparent.

She never got the chance.

"Well, that's that," Carver declared, brushing one hand against the other as if dusting something off his palms. "I just put a new case on Warner's desk, but he's out of the office on one of the other cases, so I guess it's yours now," he told her. The tone of his voice said that the subject was permanently closed. "Don't slam the door on your way out," he told her, waving her out of his office.

Moira tried one last time to state her case. "But, sir, if I could just—"

"Out, Cavanaugh," Carver snapped. "I gave you a shot—more than most would do," he pointed out, irritated. "Your 'hunch' didn't pan out. Got lots of other things for you to do. So go do them," he ordered, pointing her out of his office.

"Yes, sir." She closed the door behind her as she walked out of the glass office. It was all she could do not to yank it hard behind her. For the most part, she could keep her temper. But there were people who just brought it out of her with very little effort.

Carver was one of those people.

Frustrated, Moira crossed to her desk. She fully expected not to find Gilroy still there. He did *not* strike her as someone who would hang around for more than a couple of minutes and Carver had kept her in his office for almost ten.

But, surprisingly, Gilroy was still there.

Something fluttered in her stomach. Moira deliberately blocked it out.

Perched on the corner of her desk, Davis rose the moment she approached.

"He didn't go for it, did he?" he asked.

The question was just a formality. He could tell by the woman's expression that she hadn't convinced her lieutenant to give her another crack at what might or might not have been a case. Just as well, he thought, something akin to relief slipping through him.

"No, he didn't," she answered, wondering if perhaps Gilroy had had a change of heart.

His next words answered that question for her.

"Figured he wouldn't." He turned to leave. "Well, see you around, Cavanaugh."

She looked at him, not bothering to disguise her exasperation. "Then you're giving up, too?"

"Nothing to give up," Davis pointed out. "Nothing there to begin with."

She glanced at her watch out of habit. She knew what time it was. "We've still got thirty-two hours," she noted.

"Case closed, Cavanaugh," Davis reminded her. With that, he proceeded to walk out of the squad room.

Moira watched him go.

Well, she wasn't about to beg. She might have, if she thought she had a prayer of making Gilroy come around, but the major crimes detective looked about as flexible as a rock, so there was no point in humiliating herself and asking him to work the case with her off the books.

Moira reached over to pick up the sheet of paper Carver had told her he'd deposited on Warner's desk and then sank into the chair at her own desk.

She glanced at the information on the paper. It was a standard Break and Enter, she concluded after reading only the first two lines. The victim listed several items that had been stolen, one of which was a twenty-five-year-old, nineteen-inch television set. She guessed that had most likely found its way into a Dumpster once the burglar had taken a second look and assessed its value.

Moira wearily closed her eyes.

This just *wasn't* her day.

Because she had given her word, Moira called Blake Kincannon after she'd given herself a little time to pull herself together.

"Judge, it's Moira. I said I'd call you back."

The man on the other end paused as he quickly assessed her tone. "You didn't find anything, did you?"

"No, we didn't," she said truthfully.

"And it's still eating at you, isn't it?"

She hadn't expected that. "How did you…?"

She heard him laugh softly. "I've been married to Greer for a while," Blake reminded her. "Even the least-astute husband picks up on things after a while."

"I wouldn't categorize you as that, Judge," Moira told him.

"Well, let me know if I can be of any further help. I have a feeling this isn't over yet. When your family gets hold of something, they rarely let go until it's resolved to their satisfaction."

"Thank you, Judge," she told him. "I appreciate you being in my corner."

"Wouldn't have it any other way," he told her with another soft laugh. "Greer would have my head."

It felt odd not running. She'd been doing it faithfully for several years now, missing only six weeks in all that time when she'd had appendicitis.

But there was no way she could stake out the cemetery and go for her morning jog, too. Her system needed the jog, but the judge had been right. Her mind just couldn't let go of the fact that she was convinced something odd was happening at the cemetery.

Disturbing a twenty-year-old grave for no reason made absolutely no sense. There *had* to be a reason, she told herself. She just needed to figure out what that reason was.

And to do that, she needed to catch those two characters disturbing another grave so she could question them.

Taking another sip from the large container of coffee she'd picked up at the local coffee shop on the way over, Moira tried to will herself to stay awake. Not exactly a good state to be in first thing in the morning, she thought, although she'd been at this for the past two and a half hours.

This was her third day staking out the cemetery on her own time. If nothing happened by tomorrow, she was going to have to admit she'd been wrong and just forget about the whole—

Moira closed her eyes and opened them again, trying to clear her vision to focus on a car pulling up on the opposite side of the street. It was parking at the curb just outside the cemetery.

A car she was certain she recognized.

Just as she recognized the driver emerging from the vehicle.

Moira's breath caught in her throat. Apparently she

wasn't the only one playing a hunch. It looked as if Detective Davis Gilroy had the same idea.

At least, she assumed he had the same idea because
he was here.

Was he going in to walk around the grounds to
check out some of the gravesites in the hope of finding at least one more that had been disturbed?

She thought he was carrying something, but because of the lack of light right in front of the entrance
and the angle, she couldn't make out what it was or
even *if* she was right.

Gilroy entered the cemetery and turned a corner.
Consumed with curiosity, Moira immediately jumped
out of her car. The next second she was hurrying to
the cemetery and after the detective.

Moving swiftly passed the tall wrought-iron gates,
Moira looked around and for a moment thought she'd
lost Gilroy.

And then she spotted him.

Gilroy was walking down one of the paths in the
cemetery. His gait told her the detective knew exactly
where he was going.

Could she have been wrong in her thinking right
from the start? Had Gilroy been the one who had disturbed the grave in the first place and those two figures in black—most likely kids—had caught him in
the act instead of the other way around?

If that was the case, then maybe he'd been chasing after the duo because he'd wanted to make sure
they were not going to say anything to expose what
he was doing.

Moira didn't like where her thoughts were taking her, but what other explanation was there now that she saw Gilroy skulking around here at this hour?

Once again, her breath caught in her throat. This time as she saw the detective come to a stop by a grave with an extra-large headstone.

Although she'd tried to focus on it, she still couldn't make out what Gilroy was carrying.

Could it be a shovel?

Had he come back to finish the job or to try again? Had he agreed to work with her—acting surly—so he could keep an eye on her and make sure she hadn't stumbled across whatever it was he was doing out there?

But the gravesite he was standing at was *not* the one that they'd exhumed three days ago.

Just what was going on here?

Moira briefly toyed with the idea of backing into the shadows so that Gilroy wouldn't accidentally catch sight of her. Once out of sight, she could call for backup.

What backup? she silently demanded. She wasn't supposed to be here in the first place. Nobody in her department would respond without a good reason.

She could always call her brothers. But what if she was wrong, after all? She knew her brothers. She'd never live this down. They'd rub it in until they were all in their eighties.

No, she needed more to go on; some kind of tangible evidence. Besides, she was a police detective, she argued. She knew how to take care of herself.

Making up her mind, Moira silently crept out of the shadows. Treading softly, she approached Gilroy from behind.

"Hey—"

It was the only word she managed to get out. One second she was standing behind Davis Gilroy, about to confront the man. The next she was lying flat on her back on the ground with Gilroy right on top of her, pinning her hands over her head, shouting something unintelligible at her.

Chapter 8

"Get off me!" Moira cried, outraged, when she could finally catch her breath again.

The air had been knocked out of her partially because Gilroy had suddenly thrown her to the ground and partially because of the totally unexpected effect she was experiencing by his body pressing down so intimately against hers.

This was entirely the wrong time, wrong place and definitely the wrong person for her to be having this kind of reaction.

"Why the hell are you following me, Cavanaugh?" Davis demanded. He didn't move a muscle. He knew if he did, he'd lose his advantage and get nothing out of her. And he wanted answers.

"Why are you here?" Moira countered.

Trying to buck the detective off her body only succeeded in underscoring the very heated connection rather than lessen it.

"I asked you first and, from what I can see, I have the advantage," he told her as he tightened his grasp on her wrists. He was still holding on to them firmly, keeping them directly above her head.

Her eyes, narrowed into angry blue slits, shot daggers at him. "Unless you want to go through life with a permanent limp, Gilroy, I suggest you get off me *right now.*"

Moira shifted, managing to raise her knee just enough. To her surprise, Gilroy backed off. Whether he believed her threat or he had some residual traces of a gentleman in him, she didn't know. In either case, Gilroy withdrew both his hold on her wrists and his weight from her body.

Then, taking her hand, he pulled her to her feet as he gained his own.

But once they were both upright, he didn't release his hold on her hand. "Now, why were you following me?" he asked.

Moira raised her chin defiantly. "I wasn't," she denied.

"You snuck up behind me," he accused.

She didn't like explaining herself, not to someone like this who kept everything close to his vest. She liked the fact that her body was still defiantly tingling from their unexpected contact even less. It just made her angrier.

"I was staked out across the street from the cemetery, the same way I've been for the past three days," she finally retorted tersely. "When I saw you pull up and then go into the cemetery, I thought maybe there was something I was overlooking—" She looked at him pointedly. "So I followed you inside."

"Something you were overlooking," he repeated, growing more irate with each word. "You mean like *I* was the grave robber?" Davis asked incredulously. His tone told her that he thought she'd lost her mind.

Her eyes were blazing. He was the one who had thrown her to the ground. He had no right to act indignant this way. "You said it, I didn't."

"No, you *implied* it," he affirmed. "I just put it into words." Completely taken aback by the implication, Davis shook his head. "Of all the idiotic—"

She wasn't about to stand there and allow him to act so high-handedly when all she'd done was form a logical conclusion.

"Well, you've got to admit that it's a little odd," she pointed out, "hanging around a cemetery, in the dark, twice in one week. If you're not guilty of hiding something, why'd you react the way you just did and throw me to the ground?" she asked.

"Because the way you snuck up behind me, I thought you were one of those two characters from the other morning," he retorted.

Moira opened her mouth then shut it. When she opened it again, it was to grudgingly admit, "I guess that makes sense."

"Thank you."

There was frost attached to every single letter of

the words when he uttered them. But Moira was not about to have him turn this around on her.

"That still doesn't explain what you're doing here—or what I saw you carry in."

He stared at her in amazed disbelief. The expression on Gilroy's face all but shouted, "You've got to be kidding me."

"And just what did you *think* you saw me carry in?" he asked.

Moira would have loved to have shouted something at him, but she was forced to shrug. Looking away, she admitted in a far lower voice, "It was too dark for me to make it out."

"So that means you didn't see me smuggle in my miniature bulldozer?"

"What?" Too late Moira realized the detective was being sarcastic at her expense. "Okay, point taken," she allowed begrudgingly. "But that still doesn't answer my question about what you were doing here at this hour—twice in one week."

His expression darkened. "Sorry, I must have missed the memo that said you were my keeper."

Moira felt her temper begin to really fray—then told herself that in his place, she'd probably react the same way. Sometimes, she hated the fact that something within her forced her to be as fair as she was. She blamed it on her upbringing.

"How about just somebody making an interested inquiry?" she proposed.

Gilroy scowled and she braced herself for another sarcastic barb.

So she was completely caught off guard when Gilroy told her in a surprisingly subdued voice, "I was paying a visit to my parents' grave. This time of the morning, nobody's around. Nobody's *usually* around," he corrected, looking at her pointedly.

Moira looked at the oversize gravestone and, for the first time, read the names chiseled side by side: Martha and James Gilroy.

The dates of birth were different, but the date of the couple's death was exactly the same. They had died together.

"You lost both of them at the same time?" Her voice was filled with equal parts sorrow and empathy, as well as contrition for having intruded on him in this way. But she had done it in complete ignorance.

"Yeah."

Davis was a private person by definition and absolutely hated talking about himself or revealing anything of a personal nature beyond his name and his department. Yet this woman had gotten him to turn his back on his cardinal rule not once, but twice in the limited time that he'd known her.

"I'm really sorry," she told him quietly, searching for a way to make it up to him.

"I didn't tell you to make you feel sorry. I told you so that you'd stop looking at me as if I was public enemy number one," Davis snapped. "Now, unless there's something else you'd like to accuse me of, I'd like you to back off and give me some space here."

"Oh, yes, of course." Flustered, Moira told him "I'm

sorry" again as she backed away and gave him the space he'd requested.

She heard the detective grunt at her in response. Or at least it sounded like a grunt. She wasn't about to ask him to repeat what he'd just said. She felt terrible about interrupting him as it was, maybe even over and above what she should have felt. The man was definitely not warmth personified, and yet she felt for him. Felt something for him and, for the life of her, she couldn't really begin to explain why.

Moira couldn't shake the feeling that had descended over her no matter how hard she tried during the course of her day at the precinct.

It seemed to hang over her like the fictional albatross, never far from her thoughts no matter what she was doing while she attempted to get a handle on the latest B and E she'd been assigned to work.

And if it did somehow manage to escape her mind for a second, it would burst back on her, ambushing her thoughts and exploding like a hidden hand grenade.

She needed to find a way to make amends and to put her conscience at some sort of peace. She knew that seeking Gilroy out and repeating her apology—yet again—was useless. She already knew how the man reacted to apologies.

What she needed was to prove to Gilroy how badly she felt about intruding on him like that. She had to get her intended message across.

After considering—and discarding—several possibilities, she settled on taking flowers to his parents' grave. From what she'd seen, Gilroy was the only one who left flowers on their gravesite. For him to go out of his way like that showed her how much his parents must have meant to him and how much he still cared— even if he would probably rather die first before admitting the fact.

So, taking a break for lunch, something she actually did rather infrequently when she was working, Moira swung by a florist whose sign proclaimed the shop specialized in funeral arrays. Taking a few minutes to make a selection, she finally bought a tasteful arrangement of white roses in a wicker basket.

Moira placed them on the passenger seat next to her and drove directly to the cemetery.

It was the middle of the day and, unlike the last time she'd been here, there were a few people scattered around on the grounds.

She heard several people talking, but rather than listen to any random conversation, as was sometimes her habit, Moira made her way to the area of the cemetery where Gilroy's parents were buried.

In the light of day, it took a little doing on her part.

The cemetery had looked different in the predawn light than it did now in full daylight, but after a few wrong turns, she finally managed to find the gravesite she was looking for. As far as headstones went, the rectangular white marble was subdued yet impressive in its purity of lines and in its simplicity.

"Sorry about this morning," she murmured to the couple whose earthly remains were buried beneath the headstone. "I didn't mean to intrude on your time together with your son. If he'd told me what he was doing here, I wouldn't have followed him in, or hovered over him in the first place." She suppressed a sigh. "Your son's a little difficult to get any information out of, but then, you probably already know that," she said, placing the basket next to the bouquet Gilroy had left earlier. "It's not much," she admitted, "but this is just my small way of apologizing."

Taking a couple of steps back, Moira stood and regarded the dual grave for a long moment, wondering how she would have felt if both of her parents had been taken from her at the same time.

She'd lost her mother at an early age, which had left her feeling bereft for a long time—but she'd had a whole family that had served as one another's support system. If she'd had to face that kind of grief alone, she didn't know how she would have been able to withstand the pain and trauma.

Moira caught herself feeling sorry for the taciturn detective and wishing there was some way she could make amends—not that he would allow it, she thought the next moment.

At any rate, she had to get back. She had an interview set up with a possible witness to the robbery of the "ancient TV"—as she referred to her present case in her mind—and she had less than an hour to get there.

Attempting to retrace her steps, Moira found that she had somehow taken a wrong turn and was now wandering in a completely unfamiliar-looking section of the cemetery.

Her total lack of a sense of direction almost seemed to taunt her. She should have brought bread crumbs, Moira upbraided herself in absolute frustration.

Looking around, she tried to find someone to point out which path she needed to take to get out of the cemetery. Otherwise, she had a feeling she might wind up wandering around aimlessly for hours—if not more.

All the people she had either seen or heard as she'd made her way to Gilroy's parents' gravesite seemed to be nowhere in sight.

She had no choice but to try to find her own way.

Turning down yet another unfamiliar path, one that was very apparently in the older section of the cemetery, Moira suddenly stopped looking for the way out and stared at the grave she had stumbled across.

The ground beneath the headstone appeared disturbed, just like the one from several days ago.

And, just like the one from several days ago, the date on the headstone told her that the person beneath it had been buried twenty years ago.

It was a hell of a coincidence—and her father had taught her not to believe in coincidences.

Taking out her cell, she did what she'd done at the other gravesite. She took pictures.

Stepping around the site, she kept snapping, turning the pieces into one large panoramic shot, just as she had done before. She kept her eyes strictly on the ground in front of her, concentrating on leaving no portion out.

That was why she didn't see it until she stumbled upon it.

More specifically, until she'd stumbled on the handle sticking out from beneath a juniper bush planted there by someone from either the deceased's family or friends.

She put her cell phone away for the moment and turned to investigate just what she'd tripped over. She took out her handkerchief and gripped the handle, pulling it out from beneath the bush.

The handle was attached to a blade.

Apparently whoever had disturbed the grave had used the shovel to do it and then forgotten to take it after they'd gotten what they were after—or maybe buried?

Moira still had no satisfactory answer when it came to that. But she would, she promised herself.

She would.

Finished commemorating the disturbed gravesite with her camera, Moira took a photograph of the shovel, making sure that she also got the juniper bush into the shot, as well.

"Okay, now what?" she murmured to herself. How was she going to get anyone to let her exhume *this* body?

She had to admit that this had all the earmarks of the old fable about the boy who had cried wolf. Even with all these new photographs she'd taken, she had an uneasy feeling she would never get Lieutenant Carver to agree to let her do yet another investigation here at the cemetery.

She supposed that she could talk to the grounds-keeper again. The man had been uncooperative and unfriendly the first time around, but maybe pointing out this second disturbed gravesite might bring him around to her side. If so, she could get him to report the crime. Once the complaint was filed, Carver would have to allow her to look into it.

But what if the groundskeeper was the one disturbing the graves for some reason of his own? Or at least involved in what was going on? Alerting Weaver would really work against her in that case.

"First things first, Moi," she told herself. "You've got to find your way out of this maze of tombstones and dead people."

The only question that remained, she thought as she looked around what appeared to be an endless sea of headstones, was how.

Chapter 9

In the end, because time was important, Moira was forced to call her youngest sister, Valri, for help.

In addition to being a virtual wizard when it came to computers and getting them to cough up embedded data as well as being one of the Aurora police force's most recently minted detectives, Valri Cavanaugh was the living, breathing embodiment of a GPS system. Moira firmly believed that her little sister could undoubtedly guide a small fleet of fog-enshrouded crafts safely to shore with one hand tied behind her back.

And Valri, unlike their brothers, would not hold Moira's lack of a sense of direction against her or tease her incessantly about it for the next three decades—if not longer.

The hard part was getting Valri's attention. Her sister had a tendency to become completely immersed in her work to the exclusion of everything else.

It took ten minutes for Valri to finally respond to her text.

Once she did, Moira asked her to ping her cell phone, lock in on it and then give her directions on how to get to the cemetery's east entrance. She'd parked her car there.

Five minutes later, Moira was behind the wheel of her vehicle, heading back to the precinct.

Relieved to finally be out of the cemetery—she was beginning to feel like a hapless rat in a maze—Moira braced herself for her next challenge. She began to mentally gear herself up for a second go-round with her less-than-approachable lieutenant, rehearsing in her mind what she would say to him.

She never got a chance to use any of the arguments she'd prepared. The moment she broached the subject to Carver, he shut her down.

"I thought you Cavanaughs were supposed to be smart," Carver said sarcastically. "What part of 'no' don't you understand?"

"But, sir, it can't be a coincidence that I found a second grave that's been tampered with."

The lieutenant glared at her. "I'm not authorizing any more time for this wild-goose chase just because the guy who's supposed to be taking care of the graves there is falling down on the job."

Telling Carver that it wasn't that simple a matter wouldn't carry any weight with the man. She phrased her appeal differently. "But if I could have just a little more time—" she began.

"I said no and I mean no. Now get back to the case I assigned you—unless you suddenly find yourself needing a leave of absence without pay," he snarled.

He was getting to her, but Moira held on to her temper. She wasn't about to give up easily. "But, Lieutenant, I have pictures—"

Gripping the armrests, Carver straightened in his chair, looking some two inches taller. "I don't care if you have a whole freakin' two-hour movie with a cast of thousands, the answer's still no."

She gave it one last try. "Don't you think that it's kind of odd that both the first grave and the second grave had coffins in them that were buried twenty years ago?" she asked doggedly. She refused to believe the man didn't make the connection.

The expression on Carver's face bordered on barely suppressed fury.

"I think a lot of things are odd, Cavanaugh—like bacon-flavored potato chips—but I'm not about to authorize a costly investigation into that, either. As for both those coffins you're so fascinated with being buried twenty years ago…in case it escaped your notice, people *did* die twenty years ago. Something had to be done with those bodies. Burying them seemed like a logical solution," he concluded sarcastically. His voice grew hard as he asked, "How are you coming along with the last B and E I gave you?"

Moira suppressed an impatient sigh. "I'm still working it."

"Work harder. And stop hanging around cemeteries," he all but snarled, waving her out of his office. "Close the door behind you," he snapped just before he went back to ignoring her.

Closing the door, Moira counted to ten. She'd entered the fray aware that it might not go the way she'd hoped no matter what.

But that didn't help to abate her frustration.

Moira gave the B and E her best shot.

Three hours after reviewing the information she'd gathered regarding the ancient TV heist and canvasing the neighborhood where the burglary had taken place, she still had no answers. She decided to extend her canvas to include local pawnshops.

That was when she discovered that Aurora *had* no pawnshops, local or otherwise. The two pawnshops closest to the burglary were both located in Rosewood, which was a couple of cities over from Aurora.

The first pawnshop she went to turned out to be a dead end since the Golden Pawn Shop dealt strictly with jewelry. However, the Pre-Owned Palace Pawn Shop turned out to be lucky for her. Looking into the store through the window, Moira could make out what appeared to be the stolen antiquated television set sitting on a counter in the back of the shop.

"One of a kind," the pawnbroker behind the counter enthused when she walked in and inquired about it. The man patted the top of the set with the kind of affection a used-car salesman displayed for the merchandise he was attempting to push. "They just don't make

'em like these anymore. As you can see, it's a rare little gem." He gave the set a long once-over before saying, "I can let you have it for…say, a hundred bucks."

She doubted the broker had paid the burglar more
than twenty-five dollars, if that much, for the stolen
merchandise.

"Just when did you come into possession of this
'one of a kind' set?" she asked.

He pretended to think. "As a matter of fact, just recently. Can't promise that it'll still be here when you
come back if you're thinking of sleeping on it," he told
her, trying to seal the deal.

Moira glanced up at the camera mounted on the wall
directly above the counter. "Does that camera work?"
she asked, nodding toward it.

"Everything here works," he told her with just a
touch of indignation.

At that point, Moira quietly took out her badge and
identification, showing both to the broker.

"Aw, why d'you want to go and spoil my day, Detective?" the pawnbroker lamented.

"Well, you just might have made mine," she told
him, putting her badge and ID away. "Do you have
the name of the person who sold you this 'rare gem'?"

Looking disgruntled, the pawnbroker pulled up
his purchase log on the laptop next to his register. He
skimmed it then located the purchase receipt. "Yeah.
Andrew Jackson."

"Original," she murmured. But then, the world had
more stupid criminals than most people knew, she
thought, happy that she could finally stop spinning her

wheels over this penny-ante theft and get back to the mystery that was eating away at her. "Now, if I could see the video feed you have from the date of the sale."

The man frowned. "Sure." With a resigned sigh, the broker led the way to his tiny back office. "Any way I can get to keep the television?" he asked her hopefully.

Moira took out a piece of paper from her wallet and held it up for him to see. "I've got the stolen item's serial number. What do you think?"

The broker sighed deeply as he indicated a box of surveillance DVDs from the previous week. "I think I'd better start asking for some photo ID."

Moira spared the man an approving smile. "Good decision."

Once she located the section she was looking for, Moira forwarded the pertinent video clip to Valri with a text requesting that the man in the surveillance tape be run through the lab's facial recognition software. If she got lucky, she might get the thief's real name and, hopefully, his address. Once she had that, winding up the case would be easy and she could move on.

And she knew just where she wanted to move to.

Moira didn't report back to Carver or her squad room when she got back to the precinct.

Instead she did something she normally didn't approve of and actually felt decidedly uncomfortable about doing.

She went over the lieutenant's head.

Moira registered her discomfort when she presented

her case to the Chief of Detectives half an hour after Valri had replied to her text.

Brian Cavanaugh listened to his grandniece patiently, looking with interest when she showed him the photographs she'd taken of both gravesites.

When she was finished making her case, she put away her cell and repeated what she'd said when she'd first entered his office and asked to speak with him.

"Like I said, Chief, I don't believe in going over my superior's head, but—"

Brian smiled understandingly at her. "But you have this gut feeling that's telling you something's wrong," he interjected.

Moira flushed. "I know it must sound silly to you—" she began, trying not to trip over her own tongue or sound incoherent.

"No, actually, it doesn't," Brian contradicted. "I'm a great believer in gut feelings, Detective. Most of the family is." He felt he was telling her what she already knew—but there was still something she *might* not know, he reasoned. "You're a latecomer to all this, so I don't know if you're familiar with the former police chief's story—"

Moira knew that he was referring to his older brother, Andrew Cavanaugh. "I am," she quickly responded.

"So you know that even when everything pointed to another scenario, he believed that his missing wife was actually still alive and he acted accordingly. Every chance he got, he reviewed all the evidence he could find and kept after it—with very good results eventu-

ally. If he hadn't had that 'gut feeling' and respected it,
Rose might have never gotten her memory back, might
never have known who she really was, and her children
would have gone on believing that their mother was
dead. I think *all* the Cavanaughs became true believ-
ers when it came to gut feelings after that."

The smile he gave her spoke volumes.

"So then I'm free to go back to the cemetery and investigate?" she nonetheless asked, watching the chief's
face.

He nodded, adding, "You'll still need another court
order."

"Not a problem," she assured him quickly.

Brian nodded. He hadn't expected that to be a stum-
bling block for the young detective. She struck him as
being very capable, not to mention resourceful.

"And for the duration of this case," he went on,
"whatever path it might take, I'd like you to continue
working with Detective Gilroy."

This time Moira offered him a less than enthusi-
astic smile. She'd given him all the facts, including
how she'd teamed up with the other detective, but she
had done it to give him a full picture of everything
that had transpired until now. She hadn't foreseen this
turn of events.

"*That* might be a problem," she told him.

Her response surprised him. "You'd rather not work
with Detective Gilroy?" She hadn't indicated during
her narrative that there was any friction between them.

"Oh, I have no problem working with him," she

told the chief quickly, "but I think he has a problem working with me."

Intrigued, Brian asked, "How so?"

For a moment she wasn't sure just how much she could tell the chief without sounding as if she was telling tales out of school. She decided to tread lightly.

"Gilroy doesn't want to work with any partner—something about losing two of them in three years," she explained vaguely. At that point, she stopped, thinking that if the Chief of Ds needed anything further on the subject, he would talk to Gilroy directly. After all, working together—or *not* working together—was Gilroy's problem, not hers.

Brian steepled his fingers thoughtfully. "I like accommodating my people whenever possible. However, I also believe in using the best people for the job and, in this case, since Detective Gilroy was in on it at the very beginning, same as you, I think teaming the two of you up again is in everyone's best interest."

Moira pressed her lips together for a moment as she shook her head. "I think Gilroy might have a different opinion about that."

"Don't worry about Gilroy," the chief counseled. "I'll speak to him—and to Lieutenant Carver," he added in case she was concerned about what to say to her superior. "You just get back on the case and see if you can find out what's so attractive about twenty-year-old gravesites that makes people want to dig them up—or whatever it is that *is* going on with those graves."

Taking the meeting to be over, Moira rose to her

feet. "Thank you, sir," she said, impetuously shaking the man's hand.

The chief shook her hand warmly before releasing it again. "Don't thank me, Detective, just follow your gut—and get those answers," he instructed with a smile.

Sitting again, Brian reached for his phone as she let herself out.

Walking out, Moira felt her cell phone vibrate in her pocket.

When she took it out and looked at the screen, she suppressed a triumphant shout. Valri had forwarded the driver's license of one Robert Anthony Ullman.

The face on the license was a complete match for the face on the pawn shop surveillance tape.

"No MENSA Scholar of the Year award for you," she murmured, looking at the man's face.

Texting her thanks and a short I owe you to her sister, she felt a little better about what was transpiring.

She knew she wasn't exactly going to be Carver's favorite person from here on in—not that she'd been in the running for that particular honor in the first place—but at least she'd solved the case he'd given her and, more importantly, an eighty-year-old, retired singing waiter would be reunited with his television set, she thought with a satisfied smile.

"What the hell's going on?"

The question—and the man—ambushed Moira as she left her squad room almost an hour later.

She'd already had a less than friendly meeting with

Carver who—despite the fact that she had solved the B and E case in a rather short time span—was immensely displeased, to put it mildly, that she had gone over his head to the chief to request being put back on "this freakin' nonexistent case you're so obsessed to crack."

Rather than attempt to explain her reasoning again, Moira had remained silent and let the lieutenant rant at her for a few minutes until he'd apparently completely run out of steam.

At that point he'd ordered her out of his office and, rather than give her the usual order regarding his door, had done the honors himself, slamming it in her wake.

She was acutely aware that Carver was glaring at her through his door and that all eyes in the squad were on her as she walked into the hall.

And that was exactly when Davis Gilroy confronted her.

"You're going to have to be clearer than that," Moira said, attempting to gather herself together after Carver's tongue-lashing. The last thing she wanted to do was to come off vulnerable.

"Don't play innocent with me," Davis began, exasperated.

"I'm not playing," she retorted, struggling not to lose her temper. She reminded herself it wasn't Gilroy she was angry with, it was Carver. "Now, exactly what are you asking me?"

About to tell her, Davis abruptly stopped and looked at her more closely. He saw what she was trying so hard to cover up: frustration and weariness. He found himself feeling sorry for her, which in turn annoyed him, but it didn't change his reaction. Damn it, what was it about this woman that kept getting to him?

"You okay?" he asked gruffly.

"Other than having the lieutenant and now you yell into my face, I'm just peachy," she quipped sharply, doing her best to hide hurt feelings.

Davis saw through the flippant rhetoric. "Why is he yelling at you?"

"Most likely for the same reason you are, but I won't know that for sure until you tell me exactly what you're asking."

He had a feeling she knew exactly what he was asking, but he went through the motions of an explanation anyway. "The Chief of Ds called my captain, who then called me into his office to tell me that I was 'back' on the cemetery case. I thought we'd already decided that there *is* no cemetery case," he said to her. "You change your mind?"

Moira shrugged, avoiding his probing eyes. "I had it changed for me."

"By whom?" he asked.

"More like a what."

The other detective paused for a long moment before finally asking, "Okay, I'll bite." He was being more accommodating than she'd thought he'd be. "What?"

At least she could give him the facts. "I found another grave that was disturbed."

The expression on his face was nothing short of amazed—and suspicious. "When?"

"Earlier today."

That didn't sound right to him. "You still staking out the cemetery?"

"Not exactly," she answered then left it there. She hadn't left the flowers on his parents' grave to get any sort of credit—or even to admit it to him.

The truth of the matter was that she hadn't really thought it out, other than wanting to find a way to make amends for treading on the detective's private wound.

"I was at the cemetery earlier," she finally said, "looking around, to see if I could find something that might open up the case again. I really feel that there's something going on there," she added quickly. That was the key to the whole thing; her gut feeling that just wouldn't allow her to leave the matter alone.

"I see," he replied thoughtfully. "And did you find that disturbed grave before or after you left the roses on my parents' grave?" he asked.

Moira's mouth dropped open.

Chapter 10

"Flower basket?" Moira asked, trying to sound as if she had no idea what he was talking about when she finally found her voice.

Davis laughed drily, though there was little humor in his voice.

"Well, now I know you can't act. Do me a favor, Cavanaugh. If we wind up having to fabricate something in order to get information out of a possible suspect—if we manage to get that far in this case—you let me do the talking."

Moira deliberately ignored the obvious insult and went straight to the heart of what he was subtly telling her.

"Then you *are* on board for the investigation?" She

didn't bother to try to hide the hopeful note in her voice.

The look he gave her was far from a happy one. He still had a problem with being partnered with anyone. But when the chief of detectives issued an order—no matter how politely—there was only one path open for him to take.

"I'd say more like I was being shoved on board— but I'm in, if that's what you're asking. And before you say anything that remotely sounds like 'thanks,' I'd like to draw your attention to the fact that I have no choice in the matter."

Moira nodded. This man apparently wouldn't admit to doing a good thing even if *not* admitting it meant being drawn and quartered.

"Thanks nonetheless," she replied. Then, because she knew he didn't want to waste any time, she told him the plan—at least the one she'd come up with for now. "I thought we'd see if we can track down a next of kin for this newest dearly departed who's had her grave disturbed."

Davis went to the logical immediate next step. "That means we have to talk to Weaver again, doesn't it?"

By her expression, he judged that she didn't like it any better than he did. "Unless we get lucky and there's someone else in the chapel office."

"How lucky do you feel?" he asked her.

Moira paused to look at him for a long moment. She had expected Gilroy to be dragged back into the investigation kicking and screaming. That he'd agreed so readily—even if he'd had no choice in the matter—

surprised her. It also reinforced her feelings that she wasn't the only one who thought there was more going on at the cemetery than met the eye.

"Very," she replied.

"Then let's go," Davis urged. As they walked toward the elevator, he asked, "Do you want to drive this time?"

Moira shook her head. "Nah, why mess up a good thing?" she asked casually. "Besides, I've gotten used to being chauffeured around."

"Now *that* I can believe," Davis remarked, coming up to the elevator doors.

"Let's use the stairs," she unexpectedly suggested, going to the stairwell door just beyond the elevator.

That succeeded in getting her a rather surprised, approving nod in response.

"Don't have to twist *my* arm," Davis told her, opening the stairwell door.

Not only were the stairs faster for him when he factored in the time spent waiting for the elevator car to arrive, he also viewed them as being far less confining than an elevator car.

Moira snapped her fingers at the so-called missed opportunity. "And here I was looking forward to inflecting physical pain on you."

His eyes met hers and held for just a moment. "Maybe some other time."

"Maybe," she agreed, ignoring the sudden, unexpected flutter she was feeling in the pit of her stomach.

At the bottom of the stairs, Davis reached the outer door first and stepped to the side as he held it open for her.

"Thanks," she told him as she walked past him. Maybe chivalry wasn't dead after all, she thought, even though the man looked rather rough around the edges.

He merely nodded. "They were nice, by the way," he told her, following her out.

Moira looked at him, caught off guard by the remark that seemed completely out of left field. When he said nothing further, she prodded a little, trying to get him to elaborate.

"And by 'they,' you mean?"

Davis didn't spare her a glance. "The flowers you left at my parents' grave."

She still didn't know how he had concluded that she was the one who had brought them. There'd been no card in the basket to give her away. "Just how did you figure out they'd come from me?"

Davis gave her a penetrating look as they exited the building. "You really have to ask that?"

Was he telling her that no one else ever left flowers at his parents' grave? That struck her as sad, but she knew better than to ask.

Thinking back to the first time she realized what he was doing at the cemetery at that hour, she recalled that there hadn't been any other flowers to be seen except for the ones that he had left on the grave himself.

"I guess not," she murmured.

"My car's parked over there," Davis pointed it out, officially changing the subject.

In deference to their renewed association, Moira left it alone.

* * *

"So much for being lucky," Moira murmured to her reluctant partner as they walked into the old-fashioned, quaint chapel and then from there into the small office.

No one seemed to be around the office, but they could see Weaver through the back window, working on the property.

"We don't even know if he knows how to work a computer," Davis added, thinking the information they were currently looking for had to be on the cemetery's hard drive.

Moira considered his statement. "Well, the man looks like he's probably under fifty and I've got a feeling that he's not as dumb as he pretends to be, so the odds are most likely in our favor."

"Don't count on it," Davis advised. "He might not be dumb, but the last time he wasn't exactly cooperative, either."

Moira agreed, but that was then, this was now—and she had an idea regarding that. "Maybe the threat of spending a little time behind bars for interfering with a criminal investigation might do wonders for Mr. Weaver's sense of cooperation."

"Maybe," Davis allowed, but it was obvious to her that the other detective really did not sound all that convinced.

They found the groundskeeper doing what amounted to bare minimum maintenance by the first row of tombstones. He was raking away clusters of leaves that appeared to be newly fallen by virtue of the fact they still looked green instead of a faded shade of brown.

At least Weaver did something to earn his keep besides being stubbornly uncooperative when it came to giving out information, Moira thought.

Coming up behind him, Moira raised her voice as she addressed Weaver's back. "Excuse me."

"Yes?" the groundskeeper asked, preoccupied as he turned around. The partial smile on his thin lips faded immediately when he saw who it was trying to get his attention. "You again."

Moira flashed a wide, completely insincere smile at the man.

"Did you miss us?" she quipped.

Heavy eyebrows pulled together in a scowl. "No," Weaver answered dourly.

"Then I guess it's unanimous," Moira said, conveying her speculation to Gilroy as if it were a revelation. "Let's see if we can make this quick for all our sakes," she told Weaver. "We need some background information on Marjorie Owens."

Weaver's sloping shoulders rose and fell in a dismissive shrug. "Don't know who that is," he told her.

He turned his back on the two detectives and returned to his raking.

"Was," Moira corrected. Then added, "She's buried here."

"Lots of people are buried here," Weaver replied, still keeping his back to them. "Doesn't mean I know their names."

"Fair enough," Moira conceded, circling around Weaver until she was facing him. "But we're not asking if you dated her. We just want to find out who paid for the plot and who notified whoever was in charge here twenty years ago of the eminent burial."

Weaver stared intently at the ground as he raked harder. "Don't know that, either."

Was the man being deliberately obtuse? Or was there another reason for his stonewalling? Moira couldn't help wondering. In either case, he was making this difficult for them.

"We don't expect you to know that off the top of your head, Weaver," Davis growled at him, succeeding, Moira noted, in making the groundskeeper nervous. "But the cemetery does keep records and I'm guessing that those records are on that nifty-looking computer I saw on a desk in the office in the chapel."

Again Weaver shrugged, obviously determined to remain out of this investigation. "Wouldn't know. I'm not allowed on that computer."

Moira exchanged glances with Davis. She could well believe Weaver. She wouldn't want the groundskeeper touching anything electronic of hers, either.

"Okay," she said evenly, doing her best not to lose her temper with this man and his singsong answers. "Who is allowed to touch that computer?"

Weaver continued raking. He acted as if he was talking to himself rather than to the two police detectives. "The man in charge."

"Who is…?" Davis asked, his tone making it quite clear that he was reaching the end of his patience with the groundskeeper's so-called "innocent bystander" performance.

"Mr. Montgomery," Weaver answered, raking

harder as he continued to avoid making eye contact with either of them, especially Gilroy.

Moira gritted her teeth. She wondered if Weaver realized how close he was to being arrested for impeding an investigation. "Does this 'Mr. Montgomery' have a first name?"

"Yeah," he answered, raking diligently even though the section he was working was now clear of leaves.

She glanced toward Gilroy, wondering if it was going to come down to flipping a coin to see which of them would strangle the man first. She could tell by the expression on Gilroy's face that he was entertaining the same kinds of feelings about the groundskeeper that she was.

"And that is…?" she asked tersely, waiting for the man to volunteer Montgomery's first name.

Weaver finally spat out the name begrudgingly. "Robert."

Still raking, the groundskeeper was about to try to distance himself to another area until Davis suddenly took a firm hold of the rake's handle, immobilizing the garden tool—and Weaver.

"This Robert Montgomery anywhere on the property?" he asked, grinding out each word.

When Weaver finally looked up—afraid not to— he was almost shaking. "I haven't seen him today."

"Does he have a number where he can be reached?" Davis asked. The look in his eyes dared the groundskeeper to try to stall even for a couple of minutes.

"He's got a number." The groundskeeper's phrasing was not wasted on either of them. For what it was worth, Weaver was obviously going to continue to try to drag the matter out.

"We'd appreciate it if you gave us that number," Moira told him.

The note in her voice warned him that there would be grave consequences if he didn't volunteer the number immediately. The fear element came in when she *didn't* specify just what those consequences would be.

"I haven't got it," Weaver informed them, attempting to make one final stand.

His bravado vanished into thin air when he saw the male detective take a step toward him.

"But I can get it for you," he quickly volunteered, nervously looking toward the chapel.

"That would be very nice," Moira told him, adding a firm, "Now," in case the groundskeeper missed the salient point.

Dropping his rake, Weaver all but ran into the chapel, sparing one nervous glance in Gilroy's direction as he took off.

Davis didn't allow the groundskeeper to get too far ahead of them.

Entering the office, Weaver went directly to the desk and conducted a quick search through a large black leather-bound address book propped up next to the computer.

Pages stuck together beneath his nervous fingers as the groundskeeper pawed his way through a couple of earmarked sections before he found what he was looking for.

"Here it is," Weaver announced, holding the address book up like an offering to them.

Moira took possession of the book, made a mental notation of the phone number and handed the address book back to the other man who regarded her with curiosity.

"Don't you have to write it down?" Davis asked as she took out her cell phone. It was apparent that she intended to place a call to the number in the address book.

"No," Moira replied, beginning to press the keypad. "I have a tendency to remember things once I look at them."

"You mean like one of those photographic memory things?" Weaver asked, obviously fascinated with the very notion of that capability.

"Something like that," Moira replied.

Hearing the line on the other end of her cell phone being picked up, she held up her hand for silence in the office.

Less than five minutes later, after identifying herself and explaining to the man on the other end of the cell phone why she was calling, Moira terminated her call.

"He's on his way," she told Gilroy in response to the silent question she saw in his eyes. She tucked her phone away. "According to Montgomery, he doesn't live all that far away from here."

"Is it okay for me to leave now?" the groundskeeper asked almost timidly, addressing his question to Gilroy rather than to her.

"By 'leave' you mean the office or the cemetery?" Davis asked.

The question just made the groundskeeper appear even more timid.

"The office," he replied hoarsely, watching Gilroy as if he expected the man to lunge at him at any given moment.

Davis waved the man out of the room. Weaver lost no time in scurrying out.

"Do you strike fear into people's hearts on a regular basis, or is this a recent hobby you just picked up?" Moira asked him, amused.

"It comes in handy," Gilroy told her. Then, moving closer, he looked at her more intently. "You don't look like you're afraid."

She nearly laughed at the idea that she could be afraid of him.

"There's a reason for that," she returned. "I'm not. I grew up with four brothers. There's very little I'm afraid of. And you, Gilroy, are not one of them." Which was a lie. There was something about him that she was afraid of, but it had nothing to do with the standard definition of fear. He made her nervous—and he made her want things that would get in the way of any working relationship they might have.

Assuming a confident air was getting harder and harder for her.

His expression remained unreadable. "I'll keep that in mind," he told her.

Looking around the small office, Davis came to the conclusion that housekeeping was not this Mr. Montgomery's first priority. Granted, everything appeared to be neatly in place, but a very visible layer of dust on the desk, shelves and furnishings had more than settled in on the area.

Davis ran two fingertips across the top of the computer. He left behind a trail running across the surface.

Rubbing his fingers against his thumb to diminish the feel of grit, Davis casually asked her, "What do you really think is going on here?"

Ordinarily she thought nothing of tossing around theories, but this time she didn't want to get pinned down. Not by him. Not if she turned out to be wrong. She wanted to bring her A game when it came Gilroy.

"Too soon to speculate," she replied. "About the only thing I can say with relative certainty is that nobody's making off with body parts in order to resell them on the black market."

"Are you saying that because the body was intact in that coffin we opened earlier this week?" he asked.

"Well, that does add weight to the supposition," Moira allowed, glancing at her watch. She was timing Montgomery. "But the main reason is that both of the coffins were buried twenty years ago. Twenty-year-old body parts are definitely *not* in demand for anything but possibly building your own specimen of a zombie or whatever the popular undead thing is being called these days," she said, suppressing a shiver.

Even so, Davis took note of the way she stiffened her shoulders.

"Not a fan of zombies I take it?" he asked and she

could have sworn she saw more than a glimmer of an amused smile on his lips.

Once it was out on the table, she saw no reason to deny it. She'd always been taught to own her fears and to get in front of them.

"In no manner, shape or form," she assured him, recalling, "I even hated ghost stories as a kid."

"And now?" he asked with obvious interest.

Maybe the man was human, after all, she thought. At least he was initiating a conversation.

"Now I just find them a waste of time. The living have got too many quirks and hang-ups, I don't need to deal with the notion of walking dead people."

"Is that why you're not in Homicide?" he asked casually.

"That," she admitted, adding, "and I like foiling bad guys."

Just then the door opened and a tall, older man with hair that was graying at the temples and a small, trim moustache he may or may not have dyed on a regular basis, walked in.

His vivid blue eyes swept over the people in his office, slowly taking measure of them, one at a time.

"I'm Robert Montgomery," he announced rather needlessly.

Chapter 11

Moira was the first to reach the man, putting her hand out to greet him. "Thank you for coming in on such short notice, Mr. Montgomery."

"Well, it is my office," the man pointed out. His eyes swept over her and it was obvious that Montgomery was scrutinizing her. "But you did just catch me in time. If you'd called ten minutes later, you would have missed me. I was on my way out."

Moira guessed that she was being put on notice. He wanted this kept short. *Answer our questions the right way and it will be*, she promised silently.

Out loud she said, "I'm sorry we're taking you away from whatever you had planned for the afternoon, Mr. Montgomery, but this'll only take a few minutes."

"Robert, please," the dapper man said to Moira,

completely ignoring the fact that there were two detectives in his office not just one. "And it was just a
golf game. Coming down here just postpones the inevitable."

Moira wasn't sure if she understood what he was
attempting to infer.

"The inevitable?" she asked.

"My losing to my brother-in-law," Montgomery said
matter-of-factly. "He and I have been playing together
for over twenty-two years and I think I can count the
number of times I've won on the fingers of one hand."

"If that's the case, why would you go on playing?"
Davis asked.

If it were him, he would have given the game up a
long time ago—not that golf held any sort of fascination for him anyway. The game moved much too slowly
for his taste. There had to be better things to do with
one's time than attempting to hit a small white ball
farther than the person playing with you.

"Fresh air, exercise, they say it's good for me,"
Montgomery answered flippantly. "And my brother-
in-law pays for drinks at the end of each game. Win-
ning puts him in a good mood," he confided to Moira
with a self-satisfied wink.

"We were wondering if you could give us the name
of whoever made the funeral arrangements and burial
request for one of your older 'occupants,'" Moira said,
using the term for lack of a better one.

Montgomery sat at his desk, but rather than turn
on his computer he looked at Moira and said, "Might
I ask why?"

"We'd like to contact them if possible. We—" Moira glanced toward the other detective, expecting Gilroy to contradict her inclusion of him in this particular part of the narrative. When he didn't, she continued. "We discovered that this person's grave has been disturbed and we'd like to see if we can find out why."

Montgomery's brow furrowed. "I thought that was already taken care of."

She'd assumed that since the man hadn't been around previously, he hadn't been filled in about the first grave. That was a detail she'd intended to fill in later, once they investigated the second grave.

"Then you know," she concluded.

Montgomery allowed just a hint of a smug look to infiltrate his expression—as well as his tone. "I might play golf more than the average sane man, but not much escapes me when it comes to what goes on here at St. Joseph's." He gave a cursory glance through the rear window, which looked out on the cemetery proper. "Mr. Weaver informed me that the grave of one of our 'occupants' as you so amusingly put it was exhumed and that nothing out of the ordinary was found. Has anything changed since then?" Montgomery challenged.

"Possibly," Moira hedged. "This is another grave that's been disturbed."

"Two graves have been disturbed?" Montgomery asked, looking both skeptical and just the slightest bit concerned.

"That we know of," Moira interjected. "There very well might be more that we don't know about."

Montgomery didn't seem to be buying into her theory. "Why would anyone be disturbing graves here?" he asked.

"That's what we're trying to find out," Davis replied evenly, answering the man's question before Moira could attempt to.

The two men exchanged looks. Moira had the distinct impression that she was witnessing two elks sizing each other up before doing battle over territory.

"Yes, of course," Montgomery finally said. "Anything I can do to help. Which grave is it?" he asked, turning on his computer.

Making himself comfortable, he waited to type the name in.

Moira gave him as succinct a description as possible of the area, followed by the name on the headstone and the date that the woman had been laid to rest.

"That's before my time," Montgomery told her when he heard the date.

"The Valli family owned St. Joseph's back then. I think their nephew ran the place for them. But they left all the files when they sold the place," Montgomery explained as he conducted a search through the computer's database. "Ah, here it is," he declared triumphantly. "Marjorie Owens. It says here that her daughter, Janice, was the one who made the arrangements. I've got an address," he offered, looking further through the file. The next moment he hit the print key and the printer behind him came to life. "But after all this time, who's to say that the daughter is still there?

Or anywhere," he added significantly, handing her the printout.

Given that the burial had taken place twenty years ago, the man could have a point, Moira thought. She made no comment on his speculation.

"Thank you, you've been very helpful," Moira said, folding the piece of paper with the woman's last-known address. She tucked the paper—after looking at it— into her pocket.

Pushing back his swivel chair, Montgomery turned it in her direction then stood. "Anything else I can help you with, Detective?" he asked attentively, his eyes sweeping over her.

"We'll let you know," Davis told him, positioning himself so that he was between Moira and the man who ran the cemetery. He looked at Moira. "We've got to go," he told her.

They did, but she wasn't exactly thrilled that Gilroy had suddenly taken the lead. But because she had to work with the man, Moira bit her tongue and hadn't contradicted the detective in front of the cemetery director. Instead she'd thanked Montgomery again for his help and promised they would be in touch "soon."

However, once they were outside, heading toward Gilroy's car, she looked at the detective and said, "That was kind of rude, don't you think?"

Gilroy's response was bordering on indifferent. "He was hitting on you."

Moira rolled her eyes. "You never mentioned that you had a vivid imagination."

"I thought you women were supposed to have some kind of radar when it came to that kind of thing."

"We do," she replied. "Which is why I know he wasn't hitting on me. If anything, he was just harmlessly flirting."

Davis blew out a breath as he released the security lock on his vehicle. He had no patience with semantics. "Sorry, I'm not up on the finer points. I just know that slimy is slimy."

She was about to contradict him but instead she flashed a grin. "Why, Detective Gilroy, are you being protective?"

"Just get in the car," he growled.

Moira made no move to do anything of the kind. "*Please* get in the car," she corrected and waited expectantly.

Davis looked as if he was going to spit fire. But, after a couple of minutes had gone by framed in icy silence, he finally repeated the line she had fed him and ground out, "Please get in the car."

"Much better," Moira told him with approval.

Then, opening the car door on the passenger side, Moira slid into the unmarked vehicle. As she reached for her seat belt, she glanced down at her hand. There was dust on it where she had touched the door.

"Ever consider taking this car through a car wash?" she asked.

"There's a drought on," Davis reminded her tersely, glad for the change in subject but none too happy about having any sort of shortcomings pointed out, no matter how accurate she was being or how trivial the short-coming might be.

"Birdbath, then," she amended whimsically.

"Don't we have more important things to concentrate on than the cleanliness of my car?" Gilroy asked.

"You're absolutely right," she agreed. "We have more important things to focus on than dirty cars or slimy cemetery directors."

Davis glared at her as he pulled out onto the street then relented. He was beginning to learn that engaging in verbal warfare with this woman was an exercise in futility.

"Where to now?"

He expected her to say back to the precinct and was caught off guard when Moira responded, "How about grabbing some late lunch while I call my sister, the computer wizard, to see if she can verify that this is Marjorie Owens's daughter's current address."

"You're the primary."

"Yes, we've already established that," Moira said patiently. Getting direct answers out of this man was definitely an exercise in patience. "Does that mean you don't care if we eat or not, or are you hungry and just don't want to admit to experiencing something as human as hunger?"

He shrugged again, his wide shoulders moving rhythmically in their indifference. "If you're hungry, I could eat."

Moira sighed. He actually challenged her patience even more than her brothers did. They'd probably love him, she concluded.

"Someday, Gilroy, you're going to have to practice giving straight answers to straight questions. You do realize that, don't you?"

"'Someday' is far from today," he answered her. "I wouldn't concern myself about it if I were you."

She knew he was telling her that they weren't going to be working together long enough to be facing a "someday" in their future.

"You mean I'm not growing on you?" she asked innocently.

He glanced at her for less than half a second. "You mean like fungus?" he countered.

Moira bit back a long sigh, dropping the subject. "Do you have anything against Hamburgers and Heaven?" she asked, referring to a semi-fast-food restaurant located in the general vicinity.

His tone gave nothing away one way or another. "Nope."

"And with the resounding endorsement, we're off to Hamburgers and Heaven." Since he was driving, she gave him the general directions. "It's located on Yale and Aurora Center Drive."

"I know where it's located, Cavanaugh," he told her, never taking his eyes off the road.

Since the place was not the hub of criminal activity, there was only one reason for his being familiar with the restaurant.

"Do you eat there often?" she asked him.

Davis didn't bother to think his answer over. It was automatic and almost robot-like. "Once or twice."

Since his answer was so bland and emotionless, he

wasn't prepared for the woman's pleased expression or for the words that followed.

"This is good."

"'This'?" he questioned.

Moira gestured toward him and then to herself. "What we're having here. This back-and-forth thing," she said, gesturing again. "In case it escaped your notice, it's called having a conversation."

The look he spared her said he thought she was crazy.

"If you say so," was all that Davis allowed himself to say.

Moira smiled to herself.

Sometime in the past ninety minutes she had decided not only to get to the bottom of whatever odd thing was happening at the cemetery, but also to get her tall, dark and silent partner to become a card-carrying member of the human race again.

Even if it killed her—and possibly him.

"You do know that I have other work to do," Valri asked her when she'd placed a call to her sister while she and Gilroy were waiting in the restaurant for their orders to be filled. "*Real* work. Official work," Valri specified.

"This *is* official work, Valri," Moira protested. Because she caught Gilroy looking at her quizzically, she turned her back to him and lowered her voice, wanting to get this ironed out before she said anything to her temporary partner.

"Just not *my* official work," Valri pointed out needlessly.

"I can't help it if I'm not a computer expert," Moira protested. "Some of us weren't born with an ongoing Wi-Fi signal coming in."

"It's called opening up a basic computer programming book and doing a little studying on your own," her sister pointed out.

"Say what?" Moira deliberately made a high-pitched noise that could have passed for static in her cell phone. "Sorry, Val, you're breaking up. I'll try to get you later."

With that, Moira terminated the call. Turning back in his direction, she saw Gilroy looking at her skeptically. Although she would have happily ignored him, she knew she couldn't.

"What?" she asked impatiently.

"Your signal's not breaking up."

Technically, he didn't know if it actually was or not, but given that this was Cavanaugh, he definitely had his suspicions that she had just made the excuse up for some reason. Probably because she'd been backed into a corner.

Moira didn't bother denying it. "I know that. Val knows that, too. But it's better than just hanging up on her outright."

She saw one of the servers come out from behind the counter, a tray with a number displayed on it in her hands.

The young woman announced, "Number thirty-three," as she looked around the immediate area for someone to raise their hand.

"That's us," Moira said, rising to her feet from the booth.

She was surprised when Gilroy put his hand on her arm as if to hold her in place. Without saying anything to her, he rose and went to take the tray from the young girl.

Although on a tray, the food they had ordered was bagged rather than plated.

"Want to eat inside or out?" he asked Moira when he returned with the tray.

Rather than answer, she flashed him yet another wide smile.

"You pick," she told him.

She was trying very hard to turn this into a decent working relationship. Gatherings at Andrew's house were always filled with stories about how deep working relationships ran. She always listened on with envy. So far, she'd never experienced that sort of satisfying sensation herself.

"I'm not sure if I'm up to making such a major decision," he responded sarcastically.

Well, she'd tried, Moira thought. "Fine, inside," she said, choosing for him.

Mildly curious, he asked, "Why?"

She looked at him. Gilroy was joking, wasn't he? "I didn't realize I had to offer a rebuttal with my choice."

"Doesn't matter to me one way or another," he told her. "I was just trying for that 'conversation' thing you're so hot about," he told her as he followed her to the table she'd selected.

"Sorry, didn't realize you were actually making an effort. My bad. Okay… I said in here because this way we don't mess up the interior of your car." Then, in response to his skeptical look, she told him, "After all, your vehicle's already dirty on the outside, I didn't want to make a matching set of it by possibly dirtying the inside."

He regarded her thoughtfully for a moment. "You put this much thought into everything?" Davis asked as he set the tray down.

Placing both bags of food as well as the soft drinks on the table, he deposited the tray off to the side.

Moira flashed him another one of her wide smiles. Instead of growing accustomed to it, the way he would have thought, he found himself responding to it in ways he didn't welcome.

"I'm very deep," she told him.

He laughed shortly. "That's one description for it," Gilroy muttered.

"Oh? And how would you describe it?" she asked, curious.

He didn't have to stop to think. "The word I'd use is opinionated."

Savoring a French fry, she shrugged at his answer. "All that means is that I have an opinion about most things."

He restrained himself from laughing at her answer. "How about having an opinion on everything?"

"It's better than being wishy-washy," she pointed out.

"Well, I can't argue about that," he responded.

Moira laughed in response as she bit down on another large, thick French fry.

"Sure you can," she assured him.

Davis decided that it was safer all around for both of them if he just didn't respond.

Chapter 12

Moira and Davis were almost finished with their meals when her phone began to vibrate, letting her know that she had a call coming in.

She wiped her fingers on one of the extra napkins on the tray and then pulled out her phone. Pressing the accept button, she said, "Cavanaugh."

"You're out of luck, big sister," Valri told her, getting to the heart of her call. "Janice Owens died two years ago. I couldn't find any other next of kin listed anywhere so that lady in the cemetery has no one to put flowers on her grave."

Neither did the first person—also a woman—that they'd wound up exhuming, Moira thought, wondering if that was just a simple coincidence or if it was something that tied the two incidents together.

In either case, Valri had done her job. "Thanks, Val, I owe you."

"At this point, you owe me quite a lot," Valri pointed out, amused.

She knew that Valri was kidding, but all the same, Moira did mean to pay her sister back somehow. "I'm good for it."

"Yeah, yeah." Valri laughed. "That's what they all say."

"You know, that fiancé of yours is having a very bad effect on you," Moira deadpanned and then said, "Talk to you later, kid," before terminating the call.

Having only half a conversation to work with, Davis had put his own interpretation to what he had picked up. "Bad news?"

That depended on whether or not you were Marjorie Owens, Moira mused, thinking of her sister's reference to the fact that there was no one left to put flowers on the deceased woman's grave.

"Yes and no."

"Are you going to make me guess or do I get to pick which it is?" Davis asked.

Mentioning the sad fact that Marjorie had no one to put flowers on her grave wouldn't mean anything to Gilroy, she thought, so she merely summed up what Valri had told her.

"There's no next of kin for Marjorie Owens. Her daughter died a couple of years ago. That means we're going to need to get another court order to exhume the body."

"Which you will pull out of your hat," Davis declared with more than a touch of sarcasm.

"It's not quite that simple," Moira pointed out to him.

"It's not quite that hard from what I saw the last time," he reminded her. "Do I get to watch this court order materialize again?" he asked. "Or do I get to cool my heels in the car?"

She would have thought that once was enough for him. The man was full of surprises. "Do you want to come along?"

His shrug was just this side of indifferent in her opinion. "Might as well."

Moira laughed drily. "You really should contain your enthusiasm."

His eyes met hers. "You want enthusiasm, you should have teamed up with a cheerleader."

The way he had phrased his comment was not lost on her. "Oh, so you admit we're a team?"

He sighed like a man who knew he was going to have to remember to say even less than he usually did around this woman.

"I'm admitting nothing," he answered, "except that somehow I got sucked into this and the sooner we find out what's going on, the sooner I get back to my life."

She couldn't resist. He had all but fed her a straight line. "Because that life is so exciting."

"Because it suits me," Davis stressed. And there was no place in it for a woman who had the annoying habit of invading his thoughts and derailing them from the very straight, focused path they were on. Even if she did have a smile like sunshine. Sunshine was highly overrated.

Rising, he took the tray with its empty bags, napkins and what was left of their meals to the garbage container, upended the tray and then stacked it on top of the receptacle.

Finished, he walked to the exit. Realizing he was leaving, Moira quickly followed him.

Their partnership, she thought to herself as she stepped up her pace, still had a ways to go before it could be considered fully operational.

"I had a feeling you'd be back," Blake said when Moira was finally admitted into his chambers. "Another disturbed grave?" He asked the question as if it was just a mere formality and he already knew the answer.

Moira nodded. "I'm afraid so."

Because she had called ahead, requesting a quick meeting regarding a possible second disturbance, Blake already had the court order printed and ready for his signature. He signed it now with a flourish. "Are you any closer to figuring out just what's going on?"

Moira shook her head. "No more than before, sir. But I'm hoping we'll get some more answers once we open this new grave."

Putting his pen down, Blake handed over the signed order. "Well, let me know if you do find anything. I have to admit that this thing going on at St. Joseph's Cemetery has definitely aroused my curiosity."

"You're not the only one, sir," Moira assured the judge.

Satisfied they had what they needed, she said her goodbyes and walked back into the corridor.

Pocketing the court order, she headed toward the elevator. "Well, that didn't take long."

Davis tended to agree. From what he'd heard from other detectives, the process to get a judge to sign off on a court order could be long, drawn out and tedious. This had been like the proverbial breeze.

"Maybe the judge should start a chain of drive-through court orders," Davis quipped.

She didn't care for the joke at the judge's expense. Kincannon had made things easy for them. Related or not, he certainly hadn't had to.

"Would you rather get wrapped up in red tape?" she asked Gilroy.

The elevator arrived and they walked in. The button for the first floor was already highlighted, but he hit it again for good measure since there was no one else in the elevator with them.

"I'd rather you didn't have such a smart mouth and crack wise all the time," he told her.

"Sorry, I only come in one basic design," she told him with a straight face.

"Annoying?" he asked, guessing at the design she was referring to.

Moira ignored his comment and focused on the real reason they were together: the court order to exhume coffin number two.

She glanced at her watch. "Think it's too late to

serve these papers on Weaver—or Montgomery—and to get the CSI team out to the cemetery to dig up Mrs. Owens?"

Davis shook his head. "It wasn't too late for those two characters who ran out of the cemetery," he pointed out.

"Who you *chased* out of the cemetery," she reminded him. "I'd run, too, if I had this tall hulk of a man chasing me."

Davis frowned. "Don't split hairs."

"You're right—" She saw the surprised look on his face and realized he thought she was referring to his last comment. She was quick to correct him. "It's not too late. Crime never sleeps, right?"

"Neither do detectives, apparently," Davis observed wearily.

"Oh, come on," she prodded, tongue-in-cheek. "You sound like you're not having fun."

He stopped just in front of his car in the courthouse parking garage. Most of the spaces at this hour were empty. "I was wrong," he told her.

She looked at him a little uncertainly. "About what?"

He got in behind the wheel. "Maybe you actually are perceptive."

Moira grinned as she got in on her side. Once seated, rather than buckle up she reached for her phone again, this time to call whoever was on duty at the crime scene investigations unit. "I just might surprise you," she promised.

"I don't think so," he responded. "Not at this point."

"Don't be so sure," she cautioned whimsically. "You haven't known me that long yet."

He slanted a glance at her. And if he had his way, he was never going to. "Like my mother used to say, thank heaven for small blessings."

She heard the phone being picked up on the other end and temporarily suspended her conversation with Davis. "Hi, Uncle Sean. This is Moira. We've got another grave for your unit to dig up," she said by way of introduction.

With a surprisingly minimum of detail, she filled the head of the CSI division in on the newest turn of events.

Ending the call, she turned to Davis. "We're meeting them there so we can serve the court order and get started," she explained, putting her phone away. This time, she buckled up.

Davis appeared to be only half listening to her.

But she managed to get all of his attention as, settling back in her seat, she asked him, "What was she like?"

He'd already started his vehicle and was now pulling out of the parking space. "What was *who* like?" he asked, turning to the right and following an endless flow of arrows to get out of the underground maze. "I swear it's like playing leapfrog with you."

Moira didn't take offense. She was beginning to know him at this point and she knew he was being defensive. "Your mother."

His eyes on the winding path out to the street, Davis

nonetheless stiffened. "Why are you asking me that now?" he demanded.

"You just brought her up—that 'thank heaven for small blessings' line," she reminded him when he said nothing. "What was she like?" Moira repeated.

He shrugged irritably. "I don't know. She was a mother," he answered flatly. "What do you want me to say?" he snapped.

"Something personal," she said honestly.

He had no intentions of getting personal—with her or anyone else. Personal meant forming ties, and ties, when ripped apart, bled.

"Look," he said, exasperated, "we're working together—for a limited time," he emphasized for the dozenth time or so. "We're not socializing—"

"Oh, that reminds me—" Moira interjected as if a memory had just crash-landed on her brain.

Had he not been driving, Davis would have closed his eyes, searching for strength.

"Now what?" he snapped, knowing he wasn't going to like what she had to say and knowing, too, that whatever it was, the answer—*his* answer—would be a flat, resounding *no*.

"One of my cousins—doesn't matter who because at this point, you're not going to get the names straight anyway—is having his baby christened and, as usual, Uncle Andrew is having a party—"

"Congratulations," Davis said in a flat, sarcastic voice.

Moira pushed on, getting to the part she knew he would initially hate. Half the people who had been brought into the fold, so to speak, had to be dragged into it at first. Once entrenched, not a one of them had ever opted to leave. She figured that her family was just what her somber nonpartner needed.

She finally managed to get the invitation out. "And you're invited."

She could see his jaw growing rigid as he drove. "No, I'm not," he contradicted.

Moira decided to draw him a full picture since he wasn't getting it. "It's a lot simpler if you just say yes now instead of having the Chief of Ds call you into his office for a 'talk' in a couple of days.

"Trust me, everyone's very partial to Uncle Andrew," she pointed out. "What he wants, everyone sees that he gets. And all he wants is to have everyone eat well, socialize and have a good time. Not exactly a sinister plot to take over the world."

Davis was far from convinced. "What is this *thing* you seem to have about sucking me into your family dynamics?"

She had two choices. She could feign ignorance or she could be honest with him and answer his question. She went with the latter. "Because I think you need a family, even if it's not your own."

For her trouble, all she got was a dark, scowling look. "What you 'think' doesn't really interest me, Cavanaugh," he told her flatly.

"You want to wind up like Marjorie Owens and Emily Jenkins with no next of kin to leave flowers on your grave?" she asked.

Her question made no sense to him. "I'll be dead, it won't matter to me one way or another."

Moira sighed and, for a moment, he honestly thought that was the end of it.

He should have known better.

Why didn't he want to have someone to care about? Someone who cared about him? No one could want that sort of loneliness by choice.

How do I get you to open yourself up, Davis? she wondered. Because she really, really found herself wanting him to open himself up. To her.

"What are you afraid of, Davis?" she asked him after a few minutes had passed by.

It was the first time she'd called him by his first name and he couldn't say that he liked it—he also couldn't have said why, and that bothered him even more than his uneasy reaction did.

"What am I afraid of?" Davis repeated, as if to get the question clear in his head. "Female detectives who won't stop talking."

Her face was the soul of innocence as she told him, "Sorry, don't know anyone like that."

For an uneasy moment Moira thought the detective was going to light into her—and then he just started laughing. "You are something else again, Cavanaugh."

"So, are you coming to the party?" Moira persisted, trying to corner him.

"Don't push it, Cavanaugh. We'll talk. Right now, we're here," he pointed out.

Somehow he had managed to drive to the cemetery without her really fully noticing the fact.

"This is beginning to feel like home," he joked in a tired voice.

"Only if you're a zombie," she muttered, getting out of the vehicle on her side. "Okay, let's go find the happy recipient of the court order," she urged, leading the way to the office.

Considering how much shorter she was than he, Davis noted, the woman certainly had long legs.

The next moment he banked the thought, banishing it as if it had never occurred to him. He had no business noticing things like that about the woman who kept insisting on referring to herself as his partner. He found himself anxious to solve the case. The sooner he did that, the sooner he would be free of her.

"What have you got against us, Detective?" Weaver moaned as he grudgingly led the way to the gravesite specified in the court order.

"Absolutely nothing," Moira promised him. "The way I see it, we're trying to keep you from being a victim of some kind of crime."

"The way *I* see it, you're doing more harm to my cemetery than an infestation of gophers," Weaver complained, no doubt putting it into terms he was comfortable using.

Weaver looked the court order over intently one last time, then folded it and put it into his back pocket. "Everything looks in order," he muttered, annoyed. "But you put everything back the way you found it," he warned sternly.

But he couldn't quite pull it off. His lower lip had quivered, giving him away.

"Provided we don't find any evidence of a crime," Moira clarified.

The groundskeeper didn't look overly happy about the coda. Frowning, he ambled over to the side, out of the crime scene investigators' way.

"Everything looks all right to me," one of the CSI agents reported once the grave had been opened and the coffin lid raised.

This time, Moira forced herself to look at the body.

"Wait," she requested just before the investigator was about to close the coffin lid again. "Let me see something," she requested.

O'Shea, the other investigator who had also been present at the first exhumation, looked at her with interest. A fresh pair of eyes was always welcome. "Something catch your eye?"

She stepped around the lid, her gaze never leaving the body in the coffin. "Look at the way the body is lying in the coffin," she directed. When no one commented she said, "It's off to one side."

"So?" Davis asked, still not seeing what she was pointing out.

"So, when they lower the coffin into the grave, it's level on both sides, right? The body would remain in the middle, not slide off to one side."

Davis didn't see it as a big breakthrough. "Maybe someone slipped."

But Moira shook her head. "Hardly likely. These

coffins are constructed so that the 'dearly departed' don't rattle around." She looked back at what was left of Marjorie Owens. "This body's been deliberately moved."

"Why would someone dig up a coffin just to move the body around?" O'Shea verbalized what the others were thinking. "That's pretty sick."

"Maybe she was moved around because they were looking for something," Davis suggested, speaking up. He tried not to notice the way the woman who was currently sharing his car lit up. And he definitely tried not to notice how seeing her that way warmed him.

"Like what?" O'Shea asked.

"Best guess is money," Davis answered.

"Or jewelry from a jewelry heist," Moira added, trying to contain the exhilarated feeling she was experiencing because someone finally saw what she did.

"That's insane," Weaver protested. He'd come forward when the discussion had taken a turn in this direction and his eyes were now as huge as saucers as he stared into the interior of the coffin.

Undoubtedly imagining it filled with money and jewels, Moira thought.

Chapter 13

"Okay, what do these two people have in common?" Moira asked.

She and Davis were back in her squad room again. Pulling some strings, she had been able to commandeer a mobile bulletin board, placing it in a small, unused corner of the squad room near the watercooler. At the moment she had DMV photographs of the two women whose graves had been disturbed tacked up on that bulletin board.

"They're both dead," Davis said drolly. He was nursing a deep black cup of coffee that looked to be one step removed from solid asphalt.

Because of the bulletin board, they had decided to set up shop in this corner, using a folding banquet table to accommodate them instead of regular desks. Moira had her laptop on her side of the table while Davis seemed content with just a pad and pen.

"Other than that," she said pointedly before volunteering the first thing that had occurred to her when she'd looked at the vehicle license photos. "They were both buried twenty years ago and neither seems to have had any available next of kin. They're also both women, but I don't know if that has anything to do with any of this."

Davis seemed to think her words over before commenting. "That would point to someone having knowledge of both dead people and to something possibly being stashed in their coffins *now*."

There was one thing wrong with that theory. "Except that we didn't find anything in either one of the coffins."

Davis didn't seem quite ready to give up his idea. "Maybe whatever it was wasn't supposed to be there for long."

But Moira shook her head. "That just seems like too much trouble to go through for something that temporary." She stared at the two photographs, as if looking at them long enough might yield some sort of a viable answer. "Why not just stash whatever it is in a locker of some sort? It's less conspicuous that way—and there's no shoveling involved."

Davis frowned at her. Much as he hated to admit it, she was right. "You've got a point," he grudgingly admitted. "Did CSI trace the shovel you found at the second grave to a buyer?"

"Would have been nice," Moira agreed, "but, no,

they didn't. There was absolutely nothing remarkable about the shovel and, unfortunately, shovels don't come with serial numbers."

"Fingerprints?" he suggested. After all, if it was used, someone had to hold the handle.

"Gloves," Moira answered. "These people planned ahead."

Davis blew out a frustrated breath. "They're obviously not the amateurs we thought they were." Thinking for a moment, he raised his eyes to hers as a thought suddenly occurred to him, and asked, "What if there are more?"

"More what?" she asked. "More people involved?"

Davis shook his head. "No, more tampered graves."

She'd completely overlooked that possibility. Maybe there *were* more and, with more, there just might be an answer to all this.

Pleased, Moira smiled broadly at him. "Knew there was a reason I wanted to partner up with you. Sorry," she immediately corrected herself, realizing that the word he objected to so strongly had accidentally slipped out. "I mean, I wanted to go steady with you."

It took effort to keep his jaw from dropping. "What?"

Moira spread her arms wide. She tried for an innocent look, as well, but it refused to take. "Well, you said you don't want me using the word 'partner,' but you didn't say you had anything against my using the phrase 'going steady.'"

"There's no need for any kind of a 'phrase' or 'term.' We're *working* together for the time being. That should be enough," Davis fairly snapped at her.

"Don't ruin the moment," she warned him. Then, growing serious, she began making plans. "First thing tomorrow, we're going back to St. Joe's to see if any of its other permanent occupants have had their eternal rest disturbed."

"Can't wait," Davis muttered. Uncrossing his ankles, he swung his long legs to the floor. "Is that all, boss-lady?"

"If that title dripped with any more sarcasm, you'd be in serious danger of drowning," Moira glibly pointed out.

"I know how to swim," was his rejoinder. "See you in the morning, Cavanaugh."

So, apparently, they were back in their corners, she thought. But not for long, she silently vowed.

"See you," she echoed. "And make sure you give what I said at the fast-food place about coming to the christening some more thought," she requested.

"Answer'll still be the same whether I think about it or not," he promised, raising his voice. Then, in case there was any doubt as to what that answer would be, he tendered it. "No."

"If the answer's the same, that means you haven't really put any thought into it," she noted.

"No, that just means I was right in the first place and there isn't anything to expand on." Instead of leaving, he caught himself pinning her in place with his eyes for a moment. "Why use fifty words when five will do?"

The first reason that came to her mind was voiced. "To avoid misunderstandings."

Davis laughed shortly. "Now you sound like a lawyer. Only lawyers use a hundred words to describe ordinary, everyday items."

"I don't need a hundred. I just want to hear one," she told him as he started walking away. "That word's 'yes,'" she called after him.

He didn't bother turning around. Instead he just kept walking as he said, "Not going to happen."

The problem was that as much as he had the courage of his convictions, he wasn't a hundred percent convinced that what he'd just said was going to transpire.

This particular Cavanaugh was far too stubborn for *his* own good.

Because two of the gravesites had already been recently disturbed, there was enough probable cause to order a temporary shutdown of the cemetery, during which time Moira and the people assigned to her could conduct a thorough search of the grounds for more disturbed graves.

The search turned up two more.

"Just two?" Moira asked, almost disappointed as she looked at the group of five police officers she and Davis had been able to get assigned to the search. "You're sure?"

"We could go through the grounds again, Detective, but that's all we found," a seven-year veteran of the force named Jefferson Wakefield told her.

"I suppose two's better than nothing," Moira murmured.

"All it'll take is one to provide us with the key to all this," Davis reminded her.

"You're right," she agreed. Turning to the officer closest to her, she requested, "Show me where the graves are."

The graves were at opposite ends of the cemetery. The first was in the same section as the first two had been found. The second, however, was located in the section reserved for the more expensive plots. These faced the morning sun, which in turn meant that they were in the shade for the hotter part of the day, which was an added benefit in the summer. Also, the view in this particular section was better, both of which could be considered as important points for the family of the deceased, not the actual deceased, Moira thought.

And that, in turn, might turn out to be to their benefit.

"I take it that—" she paused to read the name inscribed on the gravestone "—Shirley Reynolds has next of kin."

"Don't know yet," Davis told her. For that, they needed Montgomery, or at least his access to the information. "But I'd say it is a safe bet. Or, at the very least, the woman had next of kin when she died."

Moira looked around the immediate vicinity. "Where is our friendly neighborhood groundskeeper?" she asked.

Weaver had been the one they had served papers on when they had first arrived. The man had looked overwhelmed with all the rhetoric in the papers so she had explained it to him, telling him that, for the time being, the cemetery had to be closed to the public and to all visitors for the officers to be able to do their job.

"Haven't seen him since we got started," Davis told her. "My guess is that the guy's probably off hiding somewhere."

She tended to agree. "Or making himself very, very scarce." Was that because he was brooding over this invasion of his "space"? she wondered. Or was it because the groundskeeper had some sort of connection to the disturbed graves?

Davis looked at her, shaking his head. "Our boy Weaver's not smart enough to be part of something like this."

"To engineer it, no," Moira agreed. "But he's definitely smart enough to look the other way if someone paid him to."

Davis gave her a rather dubious look. "Be serious. Would you trust Weaver with your secret?"

"No, but I'm smarter than the average criminal," she told him.

Davis laughed shortly. "Beauty, brains and modesty, what a combo," he quipped.

"What part of that was sarcasm?" Moira asked, pretending to bat her lashes at him.

There was something almost seductive about her when she did that and he found himself doing what he could to block it. To keep her from guessing what was on his mind, what passed for a smile fleetingly touched his lips.

"That's for you to figure out." He glanced back at

the second grave. The exhumation count was going up. "More court orders?" he proposed.

She nodded. "Unless Shirley or Anne back there have next of kin we can actually talk to."

"Next of kin might say no," he reminded her, adding, "I certainly wouldn't want Uncle Alfred dug up on the say-so of some wet-behind-the-ears detective."

"Uncle Alfred?" she questioned, instantly curious.

Did he have family, after all? Family he wasn't owning up to? And if he did, why did he act as if there was no family for him to turn to?

Again, Davis could all but read her mind. He knew where she was going with this. "Figure of speech," he told her. "There is no Uncle Alfred."

She let that go for now. But she wasn't done yet. "And the 'wet-behind-the-ears-detective' comment refers to…?"

He'd found out a long time ago that the less he said specifically, the less he could be blamed for. And the less that would come back to bite him.

"You're primary on this, but I've been with the force longer. You figure it out."

She reacted to his tone rather than to his words. "You are a cup of sunshine, Gilroy."

"Never claimed to be."

She turned toward the two officers who were closest to her. "Rope off the two graves we just found and don't let anyone near them. The detective and I are going to request permission to shed a little more daylight on this case," she said so that the officers were kept in the loop and knew what was going on.

Davis looked at his watch. It was already past noon. "This might take a while," he pointed out.

She stopped and turned around. "You're right. Sommerville," she called out to another officer. When the latter crossed to her, Moira took out several large bills and handed them to the officer. "Get yourself and the officers something to eat. We'll be back as soon as we can," she promised. "In the meantime, nobody goes near the graves—this means the groundskeeper if he ever turns up again."

"You think because you fed them, you bought their loyalty?" Davis asked as they headed toward the cemetery's main exit.

"No," she contradicted, "I think because I treated them like people, not 'underlings,' I created some good will." She looked at him pointedly as they returned to his vehicle. "I believe in treating people the way I like being treated."

He thought of her continual harping on this so-called christening she wanted him to attend.

"So what you're telling me is that you like being ordered around and forced to do things you don't want to do."

She knew immediately what he was referring to. Moira grinned at him as they reached his car. "You are definitely a challenge, Davis. But, in case you haven't really realized it yet, Cavanaughs—"

"Never give up. Yes, I know. So you keep telling me. There's another thing that Cavanaughs are," he told her, getting into the car on his side.

Moira pulled the passenger door open and got in. "What?"

"Annoying."

Moira laughed. "I'll be sure to pass that along to the Chief of Ds," she told him with a grin.

Davis started up his car. The comment he muttered under his breath was lost in the noise. Moira decided it was best that way.

As with the other two deceased occupants of disturbed graves before her, Anne Hemmings had no immediate next of kin. Shirley Reynolds, however, did. A distant nephew named Michael McFarland.

But McFarland was off on a European cruise and couldn't be reached currently. Exhumation of her grave had to be temporarily put off. But the one for Anne Hemmings went ahead.

With, it turned out, the same end results.

"I think this can now be officially labeled a wild-goose chase," Davis told her in exasperation.

Glancing at Moira, he was tempted to say something about backing dead horses, or something even more sarcastic, but she seemed far too disappointed for him to rub salt into her wounds.

He had to be getting soft in his old age, he told himself.

Davis thought back to his initial idea that a fraternity was behind the disturbed graves. Possibly, in all likelihood, that was it.

"Maybe it's just nothing more than a prank or a practical joke," he suggested.

Hardly paying attention to what he was saying, Moira squatted beside the exhumed coffin. Temporarily ignoring the dead person in it, she looked intently into its interior. Not only had the deceased been moved awkwardly to one side, but she thought she saw a slight tear in the lining of the coffin.

She examined it closely for a moment. Rising, she looked at the lead crime scene investigator. "Take this into the lab for further examination."

"And by 'this' you mean...?" Davis asked her before the investigator could.

"The coffin," she told both of them. "Look." She pointed to the tiny rip she'd spotted. "Something was put in here—and then retrieved."

"You sure?" O'Shea asked uncertainly. He examined the spot she'd pointed out. "It hardly looks like it's been touched."

"That's because whoever is doing this is being very, very careful. In fact, they're being *meticulous*." She emphasized the word. Rising to her feet, she dusted off her hands and turned to Davis. "I think that it's time to bring Mr. Weaver in for questioning."

The request could only mean one thing. "Then you do think he's in on it."

Moira hadn't made up her mind about that yet. "Maybe yes, maybe no, but he's definitely seen something or knows something he's not talking about. We're going to loosen his tongue."

"You want me in on the guy's interrogation?" Davis

asked her. With Moira, he was never really certain about what motivated her.

She answered as if there had never been any doubt. "Sure."

"Then it's going to be good cop, bad cop?" he asked, assuming he was right.

She grinned at him. "Actually, I was thinking more along the lines of good cop, evil cop. You do have a way of striking fear into people's hearts when you scowl," she pointed out.

He snorted, acknowledging the obvious. "You're not fearful."

She flashed a completely phony smile. "That's because I know your secret."

"Which is?" he asked suspiciously, having no clue what she was talking about.

"Deep down—" she poked his sternum "—there is a marshmallow center."

His frown went deep. "That doesn't even merit a reply."

"You can't think of one because you know I'm right," Moira gloated.

Davis bit back a few choice words—but it definitely wasn't easy.

Chapter 14

St. Joseph Cemetery's hulking groundskeeper appeared to be a great deal less confident and far more visibly nervous seated at the table in one of the three interrogation rooms on the precinct's third floor.

Away from his familiar surroundings, Avery Weaver gave the impression of being a fish out of water—a very panicked fish who was on the verge of losing the ability to survive.

Less than ten minutes into the interrogation and the man was sweating profusely despite the fact that the temperature within the precinct as well as the room itself was rather cool.

"Let's go over this again," Moira said patiently. "What do you know about the four coffins that were disturbed?"

"I don't know nothing. Only that you dug them up," Weaver protested defensively. He was rocking to and fro ever so slightly, his bravado gone.

"How long have you worked at the cemetery?" Moira asked him.

"Almost ten years," Weaver responded, his eyes wide, as if he was expecting to be verbally ambushed at any second. "Look, I was asleep. Whenever these 'disturbances' were supposed to have happened, I was asleep," he cried.

Davis looked at him pointedly, getting into the man's face. "If you don't know when they were supposed to have happened, how would you know if you were asleep at the time?" he asked.

Unlike Moira, he didn't bother approaching the subject slowly. His voice was gruff and intimidating.

Weaver began to noticeably shake.

"'Cause I'm asleep every night," the groundskeeper cried. He appeared exceedingly uncomfortable about making the admission.

Moira looked at Weaver with mingled surprise and exasperation. "Seriously?"

The man's wide, sloping shoulders rose and fell in a hapless shrug. "I fall asleep every night. Nothing happens at the cemetery at that hour—except maybe on Halloween," he amended. And then he regarded the two detectives ruefully. "I mean, it didn't until this thing with the graves started up."

"And you *never* heard anything?" Moira pressed the man.

"Can I help it if I'm a sound sleeper?" Weaver returned helplessly. "And these guys who mess with the graves, they don't make any noise on purpose," he added as if that served as his excuse.

"But aren't you supposed to patrol the grounds?" Davis asked accusingly.

Weaver squirmed in his seat. "They don't pay me very much and, like I said, nothing happens at that hour, except maybe a couple of teenagers wanting to see what it's like to make love in a cemetery."

The idea of making love on a gravesite was less than appealing to Moira, but she managed to keep her reaction from registering on her face or in her voice as she asked the groundskeeper, "You saw them?"

"More like I heard them. You know, some heavy breathing and then the sound of them running away," Weaver answered.

Which could have been the grave robbers, Moira thought—if she could just figure out what it was that was being robbed. Weaver wasn't bright enough to know the difference.

"So what you're saying is that you don't know anything about these attempted grave robberies, is that it?" Moira demanded.

Weaver crossed his heart and raised his hand as if taking a solemn pledge. "On my mother's grave, I don't know anything."

"Well, that's rather appropriate," Moira muttered under her breath. She was certain he would have confessed to his part in this—if he'd had a part in this. Apparently—at least for now—he was just an ignorant bystander.

"And none of these names mean anything to you?" Davis asked, turning the list of the four names inscribed on the gravestones around so that Weaver was able to read them clearly.

Weaver shook his head so hard, Moira thought it was in danger of falling off.

"No." The groundskeeper's small, dark eyes moved back and forth like loose marbles. "Can I go now?"

Rather than sound arrogant, the way he initially had when the investigation had first started more than a week ago, he was almost pleading now, addressing his words to both detectives because he apparently wasn't sure which of them was in charge and he didn't want to take a chance on offending either of them.

"You can go," Davis finally told him after a prolonged pause. "Just don't leave town. If I have to come looking for you, neither one of us is going to be very happy," he warned.

Weaver's eyes looked as if they were about to pop out. "No, sir. I mean, yes, sir. I mean—"

"Just go," Moira told him wearily, waving her hand toward the door.

Once the groundskeeper had scurried out like a field mouse that had avoided being swatted out of the room with a straw broom, Moira turned to look at her reluctant partner.

"Well, you certainly struck fear into his heart."

"Just wanted to make sure he wasn't going to run out of town," Davis replied.

Moira laughed shortly, thinking of how unsteady Weaver had seemed. "I doubt if he's able. You made him weak in the knees—and definitely not in a good way."

Davis frowned at her, obviously confused by what she was telling him. "Just what's that supposed to mean, Cavanaugh?"

Moira stared at him. "Oh c'mon, anyone who looks the way you do has got to be familiar with that expression. Think about it. 'Making someone weak in the knees' usually goes right along with a racing pulse and a pounding heart."

His scowl deepened as her message registered. "You have got one *hell* of an imagination, Cavanaugh," he told her, marveling at her.

Moira caught him completely off guard when she winked at him. "Maybe I just have one hell of a love life," she countered.

Davis looked at her for a long moment, his gaze almost penetrating.

She had no way of knowing what he was thinking or if she had managed to stir his curiosity—as well as his imagination—with that one seemingly harmless, throwaway line.

But she had. She'd gotten him wondering just what her private life was like.

And how it would feel to kiss that mouth of hers that seemed to never stop moving.

Granted she was a more than passably attractive pain-in-the-butt, but up until now, he hadn't given any real thought to her life outside the precinct.

Of course the woman had a love life, he admonished himself. She was outgoing, vibrant and could probably make friends with the devil himself if she had to. And she had this trait, he'd noted. A trait that made the person she was talking to feel as if he—or she—was the only person in the room even if the room was stuffed to maximum capacity with people.

It was a gift, he supposed, one that went a long way toward making the woman popular—as well as damn desirable.

Davis almost jolted as the last word jumped out at him from out of nowhere, all but setting the surrounding world on fire.

What the hell was he doing, having thoughts like that about a woman who was the bane of his existence? The only thing he desired about Moira Cavanaugh was to have her go away, *stay* away and stop bothering him.

Because he'd fallen into silence and he realized that Moira was looking at him as if waiting for him to say something, Davis muttered, "Remind me to send my condolences."

Well, that certainly came out of nowhere. "To who?" she asked him.

"To whomever you're having that love life with." Davis all but snapped her head off. "Can we get back to work now?"

The smile she flashed at him seemed to say that she knew what he was attempting to do and that she had his number.

All he knew was that he *didn't* like the way her smile seemed to corkscrew into his system, all but short-circuiting everything it came in contact with.

"Ready when you are," Moira announced brightly.

His eyes narrowed as he looked at her. "I'm ready," he growled.

But he wasn't, he realized.

Whatever else he might have been—and now was—he was definitely *not* ready for her.

Desperate for any sort of a diversion that would get her attention away from this personal venue they seemed to be traveling, Davis grasped the first thing that came into his head.

"We need to check out the other cemetery."

The words had practically burst out of his mouth, catching her entirely off guard. She looked at him, not even sure she'd heard him correctly, and asked, "What?"

"Aurora has another cemetery in the city, doesn't it?"

She had to stop to think for a second before she could answer. "Yes. It's a smaller one. I think it was here before they built St. Joe's," she recalled from her initial research. "Why?"

"Well, maybe some of the graves at that cemetery have been disturbed, too," Davis suggested. "If they have, maybe we'll find the key to all this at the other cemetery."

Davis wasn't prepared for her face lighting up the way that it did.

And he *definitely* wasn't prepared for that sudden quickening he felt in the pit of his stomach as he witnessed her reaction.

Maybe this whole "partner" thing was getting to him, making him anticipate things going wrong on some level and that was why he had been so out of whack lately. Waiting for a shoe to drop.

"That's great," she told him. "I hadn't thought of that."

She wasn't being defensive, wasn't acting as if the same thought had occurred to her and she just hadn't voiced it. Instead she was saying it as if she was *complimenting* him.

For a second he fell into silence.

Since he was no longer accustomed to working with a partner, he wasn't used to being on the receiving end of any sort of praise—not that either one of his two late partners had praised him outright. But approval—and that went both ways—had been tacitly understood.

Words hadn't been necessary, even though hearing them now felt good in an unsettling sort of way.

He wasn't happy about it.

Feeling awkward, Davis shrugged off her obvious approval.

"Yeah, well...seems only logical. You want to take any backup with us?" he asked, ready to call in the officers they'd made use of previously. To be honest with himself, right now the thought of having a few more bodies around acting as silent buffers was welcome.

He was surprised when Moira shook her head.

"Not yet," she told him. "Let's have a look around the place first and see if we can make nice with whoever's in charge over there."

"Make nice," Davis echoed reprovingly as they left the squad room and headed down the corridor to the elevator. "You make it sound like we're going to be dealing with a bunch of kindergarten kids."

She smiled indulgently as they reached the elevator. Moira pressed the down button. "Okay, how would you like to refer to it?"

"How about calling it an investigation?" he suggested tersely.

Moira inclined her head. "If that's what'll make you happy."

He blew out an exasperated breath. He was tired of this restless feeling that kept infiltrating his system because of her.

"What would have made me 'happy,'" he told her, "is if you hadn't been jogging by the cemetery that morning. Or, if you had to, that you'd done it either half an hour sooner or half an hour later."

The implication was clear. Half an hour either way and their paths wouldn't have crossed—and he wouldn't be working with her now.

Rather than taking offense and backing off the way he'd thought she would, Davis saw laughter in the woman's eyes.

"You know that you don't mean that," she told Davis as she stepped into the elevator car first.

She kept her hand out, blocking the beam that in turn signaled the power grid that there was something obstructing the path. It kept the elevator doors from closing prematurely.

When Davis got on, she withdrew her hand and the doors closed.

"I never meant anything more in my life," he muttered under his breath.

Moira pretended she didn't hear.

But the smile on her lips told Davis that she had.

Unlike the initially surly, combative groundskeeper at St. Joseph's Cemetery, Jack Campbell, Weaver's counterpart at Aurora's First Cemetery, was only too happy to answer any and all questions, as well as to offer his assistance in any manner he could.

Obviously lonely, the balding, fifty-something groundskeeper seemed delighted to have someone to talk to—and he talked up a storm, going on and on in response to each and every question put to him, even the simplest ones.

Campbell personally took them on a tour of the smaller cemetery, offering commentary on almost each and every grave.

And he appeared gleeful when, toward the tail end of the little tour he'd conducted, one more disturbed grave was discovered, adding it to the total from St. Joseph's and bringing the final number up to five disturbed graves in all.

According to the date carved into the headstone, Maryanne Wilson had been laid to rest twenty and a half years ago.

That, Moira noted, made the woman's grave the first in this small, artificial group. When she exchanged glances with Davis, she could see that the same thought had occurred to him.

"Would it be possible for you to look up her records

to see if there's a next of kin for us to get in contact with?" Moira requested.

She'd expected the man to get on it immediately. Instead, he made no move except to look at her with a puzzled expression. Apparently, Campbell now saw himself as part of the investigation and wanted to know more.

"Whatever for?" he asked.

She could feel Davis tensing beside her. She couldn't really blame him. It did feel as if this investigation was dragging. Still, she didn't want him to snap at the groundskeeper. At least he was being helpful.

To balance out the tension Davis was giving off, she told Campbell in a calm, reasonable voice, "We'd like to exhume the body to see if it's been disturbed or if there was anything taken from within the coffin."

Campbell's brow furrowed as if struggling to comprehend what was going on. "You mean like her jewelry or something?"

Or something, Moira silently concurred.

Out loud she told the groundskeeper, "It might be a little more complicated than that."

Campbell was already moving toward the small building where all the business that went into running the small cemetery was conducted.

"I can look it up, but I'm pretty sure no one's been by to see Maryanne in a few years."

Davis looked at him a little suspiciously. In his own way, Campbell struck him as odd as Weaver did. "How would you know that?"

"I make it a point to know all the people who come

by to visit their loved ones," Campbell replied proudly, like a sentry who never left his post, at least not figuratively. "Let's go back to the office," he suggested. Not waiting for them to agree, the groundskeeper turned and began to lead the way.

Campbell beamed when he was proved right.

According to the copious records he kept, the name of Maryanne Wilson's next of kin—Sheldon Wilson—was crossed out and a date—November 1999—was written in pencil above the crossed-out name.

It was, he informed them, the last time anyone had visited the grave.

"You actually keep records?" Davis asked, looking at the man incredulously.

Campbell nodded then almost sheepishly confessed, "Not much else to do around here." He laughed softly to himself. "Just so much raking, watering and fertilizing a man can do before there's nothing left to rake and he's drowning the flowers and the lawn. And then it's not pretty for them anymore."

"Them?" Moira questioned.

Campbell nodded. He scanned the immediate area and went on to proudly inform his all but captive audience, "I like to think of the people resting here as family."

Chapter 15

"Dear lord, I hope you never find yourself being that lonely," Moira said to Davis when they finally left the cemetery almost four and a half hours later.

Thanks to Blake Kincannon's new court order and the ever-amazing swift efficiency of the crime scene investigators who arrived on the scene, Maryanne Wilson's coffin had been exhumed and opened. It was immediately evident that the elderly woman's body had been disturbed and then returned to its place. However, none of it was done as carefully as with the other four coffins over at St. Joseph's Cemetery.

Not only that, but there were also scuff marks evident on the coffin lid, as if someone had pried it off. Recently, from all appearances, since the marks looked fresh, no more than a month old if that much.

Moira's guess was that Maryanne had been the grave robbers' first.

But first what?

And why?

Her remark to Davis as they left the grounds now had him scowling at her. "What the hell are you talking about?" he asked.

He liked to think of himself as an intelligent man, but trying to follow Moira's train of thought was like hoping a sidewinder would travel in a straight line for at least a little while. It just wasn't going to happen.

"The way Campbell referred to all those dead people as his 'family.'"

Davis shrugged, dismissing the whole scenario. "The guy's strange. I'm not strange."

"But you are lonely."

Getting into his vehicle, he slanted a warning look at Moira. "Don't start."

"I won't—" she promised, getting in on her side "—if you come to the christening this Saturday."

The days since he'd begun working with the woman who never stopped talking all seemed to run into one another, like fudge that refused to set. "That's not over with yet?"

She snapped her seat belt, the click underscoring her response. "Nope."

He jammed his key into the ignition but didn't turn it. Instead he shifted in his seat to glare at her. "Look, we're working together—it seems like continuously—isn't that enough for you?"

The corners of her mouth curved into a wide, innocent smile. "I repeat. Nope."

Davis blew out a breath. "Well, it's going to have to be. Get used to it."

He was about to turn the key when her next question had his hand freezing again. "You have a landline, right?"

His eyes narrowed. What did that have to do with anything? "Yes. Why?"

She was the face of innocence as she answered. "Just wanted to know if you're rather have the call come in on your cell phone or your landline."

He felt as if he was going around in circles. "What call?"

It amazed him how long she could go on looking so innocent when everything she said pointed to the opposite. "The one from the Chief of Ds to personally invite you to the christening."

He was getting that itchy feeling in his hands again, the one that had him wanting to strangle her. "You're like a damn plague of locusts, you know that?"

"But I'm prettier," Moira said sweetly, deliberately batting her eyelashes at him like a heroine in a B-grade movie out of the 1950s.

Davis wasn't sure just what possessed him at that moment. Most likely it was frustration.

Or maybe he just wanted to get her to back off once and for all and the only way he felt he could do that was to frighten her off. He reasoned he could do that by kissing her.

That was why he turned toward Moira and, operating on what amounted to automatic pilot, he suddenly, and without a word, pulled her to him despite her seat belt. He didn't even remember leaning against the rather awkward transmission shift that was between them, dividing them from one another like an old-fashioned bundling board. All that he did remember was that he kissed her.

Kissed her hard.

Kissed her until neither one of them could breathe anymore and the only sound within the sedan was the one created by two pounding hearts.

"Well, guess that definitely settles it," Moira said when she was finally able to drag enough air into her lungs to speak again.

This time she managed to lose him in record time. Davis looked at her rather uncertainly. "Settles what?" he asked.

She raised her head just a little, so that her eyes met his. "That you don't think of me as locusts. You wouldn't have kissed locusts."

I shouldn't have kissed you, either, Davis thought, upbraiding himself ruefully for his monumental descent into insanity. He wasn't even sure just what had brought it on—other than the plain fact that some sort of a raw attraction sizzled between them. One he neither welcomed nor wanted.

Moira took in another breath so that she could speak above a ragged whisper. "So, will you be needing that personal phone call from Uncle Brian, or are you going to surrender peacefully and come to the christening of your own free will?"

There was no doubt about it, the woman made his head ache. He had never encountered anyone so tenacious. "Just how can it be of my 'own free will' if you're threatening me?"

Moira shrugged. "That's for you to work out," she told him and he had the feeling that she meant what she was saying, even if it made no sense. "It's just a matter of semantics, anyway. So, what'll it be?"

Davis finally turned on the ignition and pulled onto the road, away from the cemetery.

"I'll come," he said between gritted teeth. It was the only way he knew of to make her back off.

Moira spared him a small, skeptical look, but for now she kept her thoughts to herself.

Instead she gave him all the details he supposedly "needed to know" to make it to the christening, which was going to be at ten in the morning that coming Saturday, and to the after-party that followed, conveniently, immediately after the christening. In both cases, she gave him the address of the church and the address to the former chief of police's house—twice.

Davis intended to be out of his apartment and gone no later than nine that Saturday morning. Not to get to the church where the christening of one Brian Andrew Cavanaugh was to take place, but to make good his escape so he didn't *have* to attend the christening. Having come to know how Moira operated, he wouldn't put it past her to appear at his door with the intentions of dragging him to the christening.

As it turned out, he was a decent judge of character, especially when it came to Moira, and he had called it. What he hadn't taken into account, however, was the fact that she was obsessively—and almost criminally—early. So while he was shooting for a getaway before nine, Moira showed up at his aforementioned door at 8:01 a.m.

Thinking it was his neighbor who periodically enlisted his help in finding her wandering cat, a calico tabby appropriately named Houdini, Davis grudgingly came to the door.

Opening it, he began his usual mini lecture by saying, "Mrs. McBride, you've got to learn to keep your windows and doors closed."

"Puts on quite a show, does she?" Moira asked wryly, moving him slightly aside as she walked into his apartment.

She forced herself to keep her eyes on the disheveled state of the apartment and not on the arousingly disheveled state of the man who had just opened the door for her. Dressed in worn, cut-off jeans that were precariously hanging on to his hips, Davis was bare-chested as well as bare-footed. His hair was still tousled from his night with an uncooperative pillow and the day-old stubble on his face seemed to make his cheekbones appear even more prominent than they already were.

He was the kind of man that caused nuns to seriously consider chucking a lifetime of celibacy for one night of ecstasy.

Davis sighed, upbraiding himself for not looking through the peephole before opening the door. Confusion always seemed to enter a room whenever Moira walked in.

"Who are you talking about and what are you doing here, anyway?" he demanded, his voice going up in volume with each question.

Since he wasn't closing his door, Moira did. "I'm talking about this Mrs. McBride who doesn't seem to keep her door or windows closed, despite your instructions to the contrary. As for what I'm doing here—" she turned around to face him, making sure she kept her eyes strictly on his face and not on the incredible six-pack she had only, up until now, suspected was there beneath the conservative-looking suits he wore on the job "—I came to give you a ride to the church."

"I don't need a ride," he informed her with what he thought was finality.

It wasn't.

"Sure you do," Moira countered.

"Okay, let me put it this way—I don't *want* a ride," he amended.

"Ah, now that I believe. Now get dressed." Both sentences were equally cheerful. "Uncle Brian made sure we had the whole church to ourselves—he's been friends with Father Gannon since they were in fifth grade together—but parking is tricky and I want to make sure we don't have to walk too far." She glanced down at the glittering four-inch heels she was wearing. "These shoes are new and I haven't broken them in yet."

Her smile widened as she could feel his resistance growing. "And if you're in need of a little pep talk to convince you that attending this function is a good idea—" she took her cell phone out of her purse and held it aloft "—I've got Uncle Brian on speed dial. He can deliver the closing argument if I haven't managed to win you over yet."

Davis bit off a few choice words that rose to his lips. "Did anyone ever tell you that you're one hell of a colossal pain?"

"Not in so many words, but I'm pretty good at reading body language." She smiled broadly at him. "And if it makes you feel any better, I've been called worse."

He glared at her. Arguing with her wasn't going to get him anywhere and he obviously couldn't seem to intimidate her.

"I haven't showered yet," he retorted.

Moira gestured toward the rear of the apartment where she assumed that his bedroom and bathroom were located. "Go right ahead."

She watched him march out of the living room and then heard what she took to be the bedroom door slam. Just to be certain, she took a few steps in that direction until she could see the closed door for herself.

"I don't know why you're fighting this so hard. You're going to have a good time." She said it as if it was a foregone conclusion.

Because he was feeling perverse as well as cornered, Davis shouted, "I *never* have a good time," through the closed door.

"You will this time," he heard her say and he could have sworn he heard a smile in her voice.

The woman was really starting to drive him crazy.

Because he'd been about to take a shower before Moira had turned up and pounded on his door, disrupting his Saturday and blowing up all his well-laid plans of escape, Davis showered.

He dressed for the same reason, except a little more formally than he'd initially intended.

As he walked out of his bedroom fifteen minutes later, he found himself wishing for news of another gravesite disturbance at one of the two cemeteries—*anything* to get him out of attending this formal thing with Moira and her family—or, in other words, half the Aurora police department.

But both his cell and his landline were perversely silent. No one was calling.

Small wonder, he thought. Anyone who could have placed the call to him was probably at the church right now.

The next moment his dark, surly mood lightened by several degrees as he was greeted by the compelling, savory aroma of deep, rich coffee.

Curiosity—not to mention his saliva glands—got the best of him and lured him into his minuscule kitchen.

The coffee aroma grew stronger and more tempting with each step he took.

Entering the kitchen, the first thing he saw was a coffeemaker on the counter beside the sink. He frowned at it.

He didn't own a coffeemaker.

"Where did that come from?" he asked, jerking a

thumb at the appliance that had just finished making its percolating sounds.

"I brought it from my place," Moira told him cheerfully as she pressed a large mug filled almost to the brim with shimmering black liquid, as dark as any storm at sea, into his hand. She'd brought both items, as well as the coffee itself, with her and had fetched them from her car while he was in the shower. "Music is supposed to soothe the savage beast, but in this case, I figured coffee might be better."

"Breast," Davis corrected her just before he took a long swig of the coffee she offered. Swallowing, he looked at Moira and saw the quizzical expression on her face. He guessed what was behind it. "The word is *breast*, not *beast*."

Her grin was annoying and beguiling at the same time, making him wonder if perhaps she'd slipped something into the coffee she was offering so readily. It was either that, he judged, or close proximity to her was causing him to quickly lose his mind.

"Again, in your case," Moira told him, "I think my first choice—*beast*—works better."

Davis drained the mug, thinking that the stiff, hot brew might help him cope with her.

Setting the empty mug down on the counter, he finally had a chance to take in the rest of the kitchen. In the time he had taken to shower and dress, Moira had not only made the coffee, but she'd washed the dishes in the sink and straightened up the rest of the small area.

Was she just neurotically domestic or trying to prove herself indispensable to him?

He didn't like either choice.

"You didn't have to do that," he told her, grumbling. There was nothing wrong with the kitchen to begin with. Clutter suited his needs. He could see where everything was instead of having to hunt for it.

"I don't like being idle," she told him. "Besides, messy areas interfere with my ability to think clearly."

Davis laughed shortly. He'd never had that problem himself.

"There's a solution to that," he told her. "You didn't have to come in."

"Sure, I did," she contradicted. "I had to come get you."

They were on opposite sides of that argument, as well, Davis thought. Nothing good could come of this.

"Why is it so important to you that I attend this thing?" he asked. "I've never been to a Cavanaugh gathering before."

And there had been opportunities. On occasion, he'd seen postings on bulletin boards throughout the precinct, inviting anyone who wanted to join in to attend. It seemed to him that the Cavanaughs were always finding a reason to have a party.

Maybe the Cavanaugh women drove them to drink, he speculated. Moira was having that kind of effect on him.

"It just is," she told him quietly, answering his question as best she could. She didn't want to get into an argument about it, not when she was so close to getting him out the door. So she changed the subject. "Where's your jacket?" she asked.

That stopped him in his tracks. "I have to wear a jacket?"

She heard the protest building in his voice and quickly offered a compromise. "Just to the church. This is kind of a formal thing."

Davis mumbled under his breath as he doubled back to his bedroom. He got a matching jacket out of his closet. Yanking it out, the hanger fell to the floor. He left it there.

"I'm not wearing a tie," he informed her. There was absolutely no room for argument in his voice.

"I'm not asking you to," Moira replied. Stepping back to take a look at the total package, she pronounced, "You look lovely." Picking up the clutch purse she'd brought with her, she said, "Let's go."

Davis followed her out, pausing only to lock his door. "Men are not 'lovely,'" he told her.

Waiting for him to pocket his key, she turned toward guest parking and led the way to her car. "Right. Sorry. Virile…handsome." She looked at him over her shoulder. "How's that?"

Davis made no answer, not trusting himself to say anything right about now. He just grunted.

Her hips swayed ever so slightly—and provocatively— beneath the light blue sleeveless sheath she was wearing as she walked to the parking space where she had left her car.

Against his will, Davis caught himself thinking that

the term she had first used for him—"lovely"—best described her.

It took him more than a minute to dismiss the thought from his brain.

Chapter 16

"Wait a minute," Davis said.

Against all odds, Moira had happily managed to find a parking spot that wasn't too far from the church where the newest member of the Cavanaugh was to be christened.

The moment she had put the parking brake on, Davis had suddenly spoken up like a man who had just had a revelation.

Moira turned off the engine and faced her less-than-willing passenger.

"Making a last-ditch attempt to get out of attending this?" she asked. "I give you points for never giving up, but I'd also advise you to save your breath."

"I can't go," Davis insisted.

"Okay, I'll bite," she said patiently. This was going to be good. "Why not?"

"Because aren't guests supposed to bring gifts? I don't have a gift," he pointed out. "That means I can't—and shouldn't—go."

The amused expression on Moira's face told him that it was a given that she hadn't expected him to remember to bring one.

"Not to worry," she told him. "I've got you covered. I brought a gift."

"*You* did," he noted. "But I didn't."

"It's from both of us," she went on as if he hadn't said anything.

Was that an intentional reference to some kind of a romantic link between them? Davis wondered suddenly. Just where had that come from? He'd never given her any indication that there was something between them. Okay, so he'd kissed her, but that didn't mean he was plighting his troth to her.

"There is no 'us,'" he told her firmly.

The look on her face was nothing if not patient, like a teacher trying to get a lesson across to an exceptionally slow child. "We're partners, there's an 'us,'" Moira assured him.

"We've had this discussion before. We're not partners," he insisted.

Weary, Moira closed her eyes and sighed. "And I thought women were supposed to be high maintenance." She tried to approach the definition of "partner" from a different, neutral direction. "We're two people riding around in a car together who, for the time being, are occupying the same circle of space. Okay?"

No, it wasn't okay. He didn't want to be here. Didn't want to be pulled, however temporarily, into a domestic scene that even remotely approximated family harmony. It would only remind him of what he'd once had—and what he'd lost. He wanted to forget about everything that had hurt, not relive it.

He was about to tell her that this was a mistake, that she could go into the church alone and he would just call a cab to take him back to his apartment. But the next second his quickly conceived plan withered and died before it had a real chance to unfold.

Someone was breaking into the moment, knocking on the window on his side of the vehicle.

As he turned to see who it was, Moira pressed one of the buttons on the driver's armrest and the window on his side rolled down, leaving no barriers between Davis and whoever was trying to get his attention.

The man outside the car had liquid green eyes, dark hair and an infectious grin.

"Hi, I'm Malloy," he said to Davis. "And, unfortunately, I'm related to the woman sitting next to you. You two better get a move on. The ceremony's about to start," Malloy informed them in a slightly more serious voice. "You don't want to be late."

"Davis, this is my annoying brother, Malloy. Malloy, this is my work associate," she said, coming up with a last-minute substitute for the word "partner."

"Davis Gilroy."

Malloy extended his hand into the car, shaking Davis's hand. "You have my condolences, Davis," Moira's brother told him. "See you inside," he added just before he withdrew.

"He seems nice," Davis murmured for lack of anything better to say.

"Emphasis on 'seems,'" Moira responded. And then she grinned. "Oh, he's okay I guess—as far as annoying people go."

"Runs in the family, does it?" he asked, finally getting out of the car.

"Get a move on," Moira instructed. "Before we really *are* late." She looked at Davis expectantly, her intimation being that she wasn't about to take a step toward the church until she was certain he was coming with her, as well.

Davis banked another sigh and fell into place beside her.

He was here, he might as well attend, he told himself, picking up his pace. Ultimately, going along with this would probably keep things running a little smoother while they were still working the case. He had no doubts that the petite blonde with the king-size family could make life a living hell for him if she set her mind to it.

The church they were heading toward was named after St. Elizabeth Anne Seton, California's first canonized saint. Structurally, it was a fairly large church as far as churches went—and the first thing Davis noticed was that it was totally packed. Every pew was filled and there were people of varying ages lining the inside perimeter of the church on both sides. There really was standing room only.

"Told you we should have gotten here earlier," Moira whispered to him, guessing at what the man beside her was thinking.

Davis appeared unfazed and he shrugged his shoulders. "I don't mind standing."

Moira pressed her lips together, as if to bite back a few choice words. "Good."

Davis didn't mind standing, but he suddenly realized that she'd said she was wearing new shoes. By the end of the ceremony he figured her feet were going to be aching. Davis caught himself feeling guilty about that and the fact that he did surprised him.

He was also surprised that he had noticed earlier that Moira and her older brother seemed to share the same grin.

This wasn't right.

He was noticing and taking in far too many details about the woman who was making his life miserable.

After that, he just stopped thinking and concentrated on listening to what the priest at the front of the altar was saying. Thinking was definitely not something he recommended for himself at this particular moment.

He had—briefly—hoped that attending the actual church ceremony might somehow appease Moira, but this was a baseless fantasy on his part. In the short time they had been together, he had learned that Moira always meant what she said. And in this particular case, that meant that he was stuck attending the postchristening party.

He consoled himself with the thought that it would undoubtedly be crowded there, as well, and because it would be, no one would pay attention to him or require him to engage in conversation. He was, after all, the outsider.

But that was where Davis quickly found out he was wrong.

To begin with, Andrew Cavanaugh's two-story house was not what he had expected. Its exterior was neither showy nor impressive. But it wasn't ordinary, either, because it exuded a kind of infectious warmth even before Davis had a chance to enter the house.

The very walls seemed welcoming and the impression only grew more so once the front door was opened and he walked inside.

Davis experienced the uncanny notion that he was being hugged—which was, he told himself, a completely impossible phenomenon—and yet he couldn't shake it.

The second Davis stepped inside the foyer, someone was standing there to greet him—presumably "them," he thought since he was fairly certain no one inside the house knew who he was.

But the tall, distinguished-looking, silver-haired man focused his attention on him rather than on Moira.

"Thank you for coming." The deep baritone voice rumbled sincerely as the man took his hand and shook it heartily. "I'm Andrew Cavanaugh," the man identified himself. "And we haven't formally met yet."

Davis almost said that they hadn't met informally, either, but a gut instinct prevented him from saying so out loud. He had the impression that the official family patriarch made a point of knowing everyone who was part of the Aurora police force, despite the fact that he hadn't been the chief of police there for years.

"Police chiefs don't retire or die," Moira whispered into Davis's ear. "They just continue into forever."

The completely unexpected close contact sent a hot, sizzling arrow zipping down his spine, although Davis did his best not to react in any manner.

Instead he focused exclusively on Andrew, returning the man's handshake and telling him, "It's an honor to meet you, sir."

Andrew laughed. "I don't know about 'honor,' son," he replied, "but it's a pleasure to meet you. I'm very glad that Moira managed to talk you into coming. There are only two rules here," Andrew went on to tell his first-time guest. "Eat and enjoy yourself. Moira," he said, turning to his grandniece, "I leave him in your very capable hands. Oh, and as far as the food goes," he said, addressing Davis one last time before he went on to his other guests, "if you don't see what you like—ask." He smiled encouragingly.

"You would not believe the size of the man's auxiliary refrigerator," Moira told him, guiding Davis toward the rear of the house and the half-acre backyard just beyond the French doors. "The first time I saw it, the stainless-steel door threw me. I thought it was the entrance to another room. But that's where he keeps all the extra food he uses for the gatherings, large or small."

Davis sincerely doubted she was telling him the truth.

And yet, there were all these banquet-style folding tables spread out on either side of the backyard. Every square inch had dishes piled high with all sorts of different foods, prepared in a variety of ways.

"How can the man afford all this food?" Davis asked in disbelief as he took in the overwhelming sight. There were people everywhere, talking, laughing, eating and, above all, having a good time.

It looked like something out of a feel-good movie, Davis thought. Scenes like this didn't exist, and yet, here he was, in the middle of one.

"Everyone contributes," Moira said matter-of-factly, answering his question. "Sometimes, Uncle Andrew even lets someone else bring an appetizer or a dessert if they really want to." At least, that was what she had heard. "But for the most part, he prepared everything that you see."

"Uncle Andrew loves to cook," said a very attractive blonde who came up behind Davis just then. "It's his passion. Hi, I'm Kelly," she said. "Moira's older sister. You must be Davis."

Shaking her hand, Davis slanted a glance at his not-temporary-enough partner. It was easy to see that he was wondering just how his name seemed to be getting around this way.

Moira spread her hands wide in a gesture of pure innocence. "I never said a word to anyone," she protested.

"She didn't," Kelly told him, backing up her younger sister. "Word seems to always spread fast at the precinct. But then, you probably already know all about that."

"No, he doesn't," Moira told her sister before Davis could respond to her assumption. "He doesn't spend much time talking—on or off the job."

Kelly gave him a very knowing look. "That's going to have to change if you want to have a prayer of surviving around my sister," she advised. And then she winked as she added, "Trust me on that." She paused to look around for a moment. "Well, I'd better go find my other half before he stuffs himself to the point of exploding. Kane," she confided before disengaging, "can't resist Uncle Andrew's cooking."

"Nobody can," Moira added for Davis's benefit. "The man's cooking is just out of this world—certainly the best I've ever tasted. This is *not* the place to start a diet," she assured him.

This was also not the place, Davis quickly found out, to attempt to be an island and isolate himself in any manner, shape or form. There was no place to go for solitude. He quickly began to feel that there was a sign on his back that said Talk to Me because so many people—people he didn't know by sight when he arrived—did just that.

They engaged him in conversations, sometimes one-on-one, sometimes en masse, asking his opinions on various topics and sharing stories of events that occurred both on and off the job.

No matter where he wandered, throughout the vari-

ous different rooms in the house or around the backyard, there was always someone who would talk to
him. A good deal of the time when they did, they acted
as if he were an old friend they had just lost temporarily contact with—and were now making up for lost
time.

By the time the cake—an incredibly tall, multitiered
French-vanilla-and-strawberry-cream-filled confec-
tion with pale pink cream-cheese frosting—was cut,
a completely stunned and overwhelmed Davis looked
at Moira in abject wonder. He had just been overrun
and conquered by a small, independent country—and
everyone was so nice, he couldn't find fault with them.

"Something wrong?" she asked as they lined up for
a piece of cake. Silently, she braced herself, really surprised that he hadn't been won over by her gregarious
family members.

He didn't answer her question with a yes or no. Instead he asked, "Are they always like this?"

"No," she admitted, doing her best to keep a straight
face. "This is probably one of the more subdued parties."

Ordinarily, he could tell if someone was pulling his
leg. But then, up until this morning, he hadn't believed
that members of a family could behave in such a personal, warm manner when dealing with a stranger. And
yet, he'd witnessed nothing else all day.

Just to be on the safe side, Davis attempted to pin
her down. "You're kidding."

For some reason the grin that flashed across her lips
wasn't annoying the way he would have expected it

to be. The same was true of the way her eyes seemed to laugh at him.

"Yes, I am," Moira admitted. "And, yes, they are *always* like this. Sometimes even more so. This is family at its finest," she told him proudly. She loved each and every member of this family. "Don't get me wrong," she quickly added, knowing how Davis's mind worked. "They're not syrupy and you won't go into a sugar coma around any of them. They're a tough bunch when they need to be, but they're loyal and loving, and I am so thrilled we found them."

Davis looked at her, confused. What did she mean "found them"? It didn't make any sense. "You want to explain that last part?"

She kept forgetting that he was a newcomer to all this—and a reluctant one at that. He seemed to be coming around a bit now, she thought, well pleased.

"Sure. A number of us are latecomers to the party." She could see by his expression that nothing had gotten any clearer for him with that line. She tried again. "There was a whole branch—me included—who lived in another city about fifty miles from Aurora."

She took a breath. She was getting ahead of herself. "Let me start at the beginning," she suggested. "Andrew's father, Shamus, had a younger brother. Shamus's parents were divorced—a really big deal in those days," she said as a sidebar. "And when they split up, they each took one of their sons with them. Shamus lost track of his brother and eventually assumed he was dead.

"A couple of years ago, Uncle Andrew looked into

the matter for his father and found this whole swarm of Cavanaughs no one knew existed. The really funny thing is, the so-called 'missing' branch also went into law enforcement. Maybe it's a Cavanaugh calling," she ventured with a dismissive shrug.

"Anyway, once the discovery was made, the members of the 'missing' branch slowly began to migrate here to Aurora, to reunite the family, so to speak. Besides, it's nicer here." She flashed a grin again, her eyes lighting up with humor. "Eventually, we'll probably take over the entire city—so my advice to you is that you had better learn to be nice to me. It might just pay off in the long run."

"I *am* nice to you," Davis informed her. When she looked at him skeptically, he pointed out the obvious. "I'm here, aren't I?"

At the front of the line now, Moira laughed as she accepted her slice of the cake and turned around to face Davis. "Can't argue with that."

But she would undoubtedly try, Davis thought. As surely as the sun came up in the morning, he was certain she would undoubtedly try.

Chapter 17

It was close to midnight by the time Moira pulled her car into guest parking in Davis's garden apartment complex. Even she was surprised at the lateness of the hour.

Initially she'd hoped she could get Davis to spend about three, possibly four, hours at the celebration. When four hours had come and then gone, she'd said nothing, deciding to leave it up to Davis to raise the subject of leaving the party.

After more time had passed and Davis still hadn't said anything about wanting to leave, she'd relaxed and eventually lost track of time.

It wasn't until eleven o'clock, after more than half the people attending the christening party had said their goodbyes, that Davis finally turned to her and said, "Maybe we should be going, too."

Moira had spread her hands wide. "You're the one calling the shots," she'd told him.

To which Davis had responded with a very hearty "Ha!" before he started taking his leave.

It took almost twenty-five minutes for them to finally get to the front door. Even though half the people had already gone home, that still left a great many others to say goodbye to. Leave-taking, it turned out, was rather exhausting if no one was to be left out.

Grateful beyond words that it had gone even better than she'd hoped for, she'd happily granted Davis an island of silence during the drive to his apartment.

When she pulled up into the parking space and got out, she finally decided to say something about the day they had just spent together.

"Admit it," she coaxed as she closed her own door and then rounded the trunk to join him on the passenger side, "you had fun."

He shrugged. "It was okay."

Moira covered her heart with her hands, as if to try to still the wild palpitations that had suddenly begun in response to his reaction.

"Oh, please, Detective Gilroy, contain your enthusiasm," she pleaded as she proceeded to lay her wrist across her forehead like a heroine in an old-fashioned melodrama.

They'd just reached his door and he turned to face her. Davis was well aware that she had gone out of her way to get him to enjoy himself and he really did appreciate that, even if he wasn't able to show it. But she had to understand something about him. He just wasn't built that way.

"Look, I never get excited about anything," he told her flatly.

"Never?" she asked, widening her eyes in that way he found utterly captivating. It didn't help that she moved a little closer to him, either. There wasn't much space between them to begin with. "So you're telling me that you're completely self-contained. Should I take that as a challenge?" she asked, turning her face up to his.

A strong, compelling urge to kiss her corkscrewed through him and he had to clamp down hard to keep it from getting the better of him.

In what amounted to a last-ditch effort to put her off, he asked, with an accusatory, belittling edge in his voice, "Just why are you walking me to my door?"

She paused, as if to seriously consider his question before giving him an answer. "I picked you up. I figured it was only right that I put you back."

Inserting his key in the lock, Davis opened the door to his apartment. "You mean like some kind of toy you took off a shelf?"

Her eyes met his.

For a split second her breath just seemed to freeze in midjourney in her chest.

"Nobody would *ever* think of you as a toy," she finally told him, her voice coming out in a barely audible whisper.

He didn't remember turning the doorknob, didn't

really remember closing the door behind them, but, reflecting back on it later, he was grateful that at least he'd had the presence of mind to do so.

Or maybe some peripheral things had just gone on automatic pilot.

What he did remember was the lightning-swift desire that went through him with the speed of a Texas twister, taking him prisoner.

Or maybe *she* was the one who had taken him prisoner and desire was just as much a hostage of the whole thing as he was. He wasn't thinking clearly enough to know the answer to that.

If he *had* been thinking clearly, he wouldn't have done what he had.

He wouldn't have kissed her as if the end of the world was right behind his door waiting to annihilate them—or at least him. He wouldn't have kissed Moira at all. What he would have done was quickly push her across the threshold and shut the door as fast and as hard as he could.

Then, maybe, he could have saved himself.

He had only himself to blame for what had happened next. Him and maybe magic because only magic could have transformed him as quickly from being a rational, sane and reasonably cautious man to a reckless daredevil, the kind who dove headfirst from the top of a twenty-five-foot-high diving board into a tumbler of water.

Magic most definitely had to be involved because he found that the more he kissed Moira, the more he *wanted* to kiss Moira. He had never been the type to overindulge. If he had a flaw, it was that he had a tendency to overthink things. Since reaching adolescence—and losing his parents—he had never just given himself up to pleasure or to any other emotion for that matter.

But today had been different almost from the moment he had walked into Andrew Cavanaugh's house. Without fully understanding why, he had just begun reacting differently to things. He certainly hadn't been able—or inclined—to withdraw into himself the way he normally did.

And thinking at all, much less deeply, just hadn't been part of the process.

What had this woman done to him? he now wondered. And why didn't he really care? But the simple truth was that he didn't. He was enjoying this emotional roller-coaster ride with its exhilarating highs and lows. Actually enjoying it and wanting nothing more than to have it continue.

Framing Moira's deceptively delicate oval face with his powerful hands, he kissed her over and over again, moving—again, without any memory of it—from the front door through the kitchenette and finally into his bedroom.

The path was littered with clothing. His. Hers. It was all tangled with one another and only a hazy memory of how the articles initially came off lingered in the faraway perimeter of his mind.

After so much restraint, Davis desperately needed this release, *needed* to be doing this.

With her.

Not just with any woman, but with her.

It was also a fact that he intended to take with him to his grave. It was *not* something he ever wanted her to know.

But for now, there were no real thoughts of safeguards. All he wanted to do was to make love with her.

He was convinced he was crazy.

He didn't care.

In all honesty, Moira hadn't known where any of this was going when she'd gotten out of her car and walked with Davis to the door of his apartment. She'd just known that she'd wanted to spend more time with him, even if that "more time" just amounted to a few extra minutes.

It was still more than just dropping him off in the parking lot and then taking off.

Once at his door she'd just gone with whatever followed, not thinking it through, definitely not being cautious.

She hadn't expected them to turn into Romeo and Juliet—especially not in light of the way that had ended for the duo. But neither had she thought of them as the embodiment of the Hatfields and the McCoys, given the attraction she'd felt shimmering between them.

The attraction she could almost reach out and grasp in her hand.

So when Davis suddenly pulled her to him and kissed her hard, with feeling, Moira kissed back, reveling in the sensation but determined not to just be a passive recipient. She gave as good as she got and for that, she got more.

Her head spinning, she could feel Davis's strong hands on her body, could feel him tugging on the zipper at her back. And then he was peeling away her dress as if it was the wrapping paper that kept an extra-special gift from being viewed.

As the material fell away, her body heated in high anticipation, wanting to feel the touch of his hands on her naked body. And when she did, Moira was close to bursting into flame.

The next moment they were tumbling onto his bed, a tangle of naked limbs and full-blown desires. She thought her heart would pound straight out of her chest, especially as his lips trailed along every uncovered inch of her body.

Aching, arching against him, Moira absorbed every sensation Davis created, every nuance that danced along her skin, moving her ever closer to the ultimate moment.

Forcing herself to give rather than to just receive, she had a feeling she surprised Davis by turning the tables on him. She deliberately shifted their positions so that, for the moment, she was on top of him.

Davis's body responded to the reversal. His desire for her grew and hardened.

That only excited her more, which, in turn, did the same for him, judging from the way his body shifted against her.

Toward the end, it was hard for Davis to say which of them wanted the other more. He derived a great deal of satisfaction from the fact that he was exciting her to this pinnacle, and that same sense of satisfaction doubled when she strove to pleasure him, as well.

Somewhere in the back of Davis's mind was the realization that although he'd experienced lovemaking a number of times before, the experience had never reached this height before, nor had the satisfaction ever promised to be as immense and overwhelming to this degree.

As a matter of fact, what it had promised prior to tonight was disappointment.

Disappointment was no longer on the roster tonight.

Unable to hold himself in check even a second longer, mindful of desperately wanting to share this experience with her, Davis pulled her beneath him.

Covering her body with his and firmly capturing her mouth with his own, he entered her—not hard or possessively, but as if they were equal partners in what had just gone before and what was still to come.

It was a complete change for him. He tried not to dwell on it.

Moving his hips in a rhythmic, ever-increasing tempo, Davis lost himself within her—something he had just assumed, heretofore, was impossible for him to do even if he *had* wanted it—which, until now, he hadn't.

But he did it this time. He lost himself in her, without thought, without plan. It just happened.

The speed—and lure of what was happening between them—increased exponentially until the final explosion encompassed them both. Davis held on to her as hard as he could, trying his best to steady his breathing and wishing, irrationally, that what he was feeling would just go on indefinitely—until he finally expired.

But even as he wished it, he knew it was nothing more than pure fantasy.

He could feel her heart hammering against him and the very fact filled him with what he eventually identified as tenderness—something he hadn't experienced in so long, he had forgotten how it felt.

Again he wondered about the transformation she had caused him to undergo—and if there was a cure for it. It was something definitely to look into. Later.

When Moira finally raised her head to look at him, he hadn't a clue what would come out of her mouth, which in turn left him utterly at a loss as to how he would respond.

He didn't have long to wait.

"*Now* will you admit you had fun?"

That was the *last* thing he had expected Moira to say.

Davis started to laugh. Laugh so hard that for a couple of seconds, he had trouble catching his breath.

At the very least, he was unable to answer her.

So Moira answered for him. "I guess that's a yes," she decided. "I should have made you attend one of Uncle Andrew's parties the first moment I laid eyes on you."

The woman was impossibly crazy, Davis thought. How did someone reason with a person who was impossibly crazy? The answer left him at a loss, so he didn't even bother trying to form it.

Instead he lay there, in his bed, in the dark bed-room, stroking Moira's silky hair as she lay curled up against him, her face pressed to his chest.

Eventually he collected his thoughts and common sense made a momentary reappearance. "The party was today, how could you have invited me two weeks ago?"

She raised her head ever so slightly, her mouth less than a hairbreadth from his. As she spoke, her lips kept brushing his.

"The man has his doors open to friends and family twenty-four-seven. There's always something ready to eat, always a place at the table to sit and always, always, a welcome in that house."

"Seems impossible," Davis replied, trying to cling to logic even as his eyes began feeling progressively heavier with each passing moment.

"The best things usually are," Moira replied. She punctuated her sentence with a quick, deep kiss.

Less than half a second ago he was falling asleep. But that wasn't the case any longer. As passion made a sudden, strong reappearance in his veins, Davis dis-covered a hidden cache of energy that allowed him to make love with the woman in his bed all over again.

So he did.

Chapter 18

When Davis looked back on it the following Monday morning, Sunday seemed like a complete haze. More to the point, it felt as if a page had been torn out of someone else's life story.

A person who actually *had* a life instead of an existence. And while that didn't describe what he actually had, Davis had to admit that while it lasted, it had been very, very nice.

Sunday had been spent, for the most part, in bed, with only occasional side trips to the kitchen for food to feed the body. Food to feed the soul, however, was obtained entirely within the very limited parameters of his bed.

Because of Moira.

Moira, to his never-ending surprise, turned out to

be nothing short of a wonder with a whole host of hidden talents. Until he had made love with her, he'd had no idea that the human body could flex that way or assume that many different positions.

But not only did she astonish him in his bed, Moira also managed to amaze him in his kitchen, as well. She worked nothing short of magic with the limited amount of things he had available in his refrigerator and in his small pantry.

"You're going to have to go shopping for food," she'd told him late Sunday night as she'd used the last of his eggs to create something that was half an omelet, half a frittata. He'd watched, mesmerized, as she'd thrown together bits and pieces of ingredients he would have never thought to put even *near* one another, much less combine.

"I might also have to go shopping for a new body," he'd countered, allowing himself, in a moment of weakness, to kiss the top of her head. He'd promised himself that, come morning, everything would go back to business as usual. But for that isolated point in time, he was going to enjoy this parallel life he had stumbled into. "I think mine's about worn out."

She'd smiled up at him then, that wicked smile that seemed to go straight to his gut, making him want her more than the very air he breathed.

"Oh, I think the warranty on it might still be good for a few more rounds."

And then, right there in his crammed, minuscule kitchen, just to prove she was right, she'd put her theory to the test.

He'd remembered thinking that he had *definitely* slipped into a parallel universe, one he really didn't want to leave.

Davis doubted that he'd gotten more than a couple of hours sleep from Saturday night to Monday morning.

Walking into the robbery squad room, he was definitely not operating on a full head of steam.

She, however, he'd noted when she came in afterward, seemed to be no different this morning than she was on any other morning.

That settled it, Davis decided as he filled his cup with the black goo the precinct passed off as coffee. The woman was definitely a witch. There was no other explanation for any of the things that had happened in the past forty-eight hours.

She was a witch and she'd cast her spell on him.

"Here," Moira declared quietly, putting a silver thermos on the table they were sharing.

"What's that?" Davis nodded toward the thermos, leaving it where it was.

"It's coffee, not poison," she told him. "I fixed you a couple of cups' worth when I swung by my place and got coffee before coming here. I had a feeling you'd need it," she told him, flashing a knowing smile.

Leaving his apartment early, she'd taken her coffeemaker with her, gone home to shower and change. She'd needed to put on clothes that were more appropriate for the precinct than the dress she had worn to the christening—and taken off at his place.

Personally, Davis thought, taking a long, appreciative sip of the black coffee she'd brought in, he preferred seeing Moira padding around in his undershirt and wearing nothing else.

This has to stop, he upbraided himself in the next moment as he banished images of the way she'd looked yesterday. He couldn't allow himself to think like that.

He was a professional, not some love-struck adolescent.

If he lost sight of the structure he'd put in place for himself, it would ultimately put everything else into jeopardy.

His hand tightened on the thermos. "This doesn't change anything," he told her in a low, gravelly voice that was only audible for the couple of feet that existed between them.

"Oh, I don't know. A good, strong cup of coffee has been known to make the future look a lot better."

"I don't mean the coffee," he fairly snarled. "I mean—everything else," he finally managed to say, refusing to resort to labels. They both knew what had gone on this weekend after the christening.

To his surprise Moira shrugged almost indifferently. "What's to change?" she asked him innocently. "Everything's just the way it was." And then she turned her attention to the board. "What's important is that we're running out of our grace period and we still really haven't got a clue why someone's messing with these graves."

Davis didn't know whether to be relieved or disturbed by her indifferent manner regarding the weekend they had just spent together. His ambivalent feelings alone told him he wasn't firing on all four cylinders. She had definitely messed up his head and he couldn't allow that to happen.

With effort, he forced himself to focus on the case. She was right. Everything else had to be put on hold for now.

Maybe by the time he could revisit the subject, it would have taken care of itself.

Leaning back in his chair, Davis stared into the inky liquid within the thermos for a moment. "Maybe we're going about this the wrong way," he suggested when he looked up again.

Moira moved closer, ready to go with anything. "I'm listening."

Davis looked over at the photos on the bulletin board. There were short histories beneath each woman's photograph, which Moira had managed to scrounge up. "Maybe these five women have something in common that links them together, something that might finally lead us to an answer."

Because she had trouble sitting still, Moira rose and walked over to the board. She surveyed the photos as she moved from one end of it to the other. As she spoke, she reviewed all the things they had already discounted earlier.

"Well, they weren't related, weren't friends, weren't all in approximately the same age bracket and, while they all lived in Aurora, didn't live that close to one another. They also didn't work for the same company or even in the same building. And they all died on different dates." That, in turn, ruled out a common disaster, she thought. Bedeviled, she looked at Davis. "They weren't even all buried in the same cemetery, so what am I missing?"

Davis blew out a breath as he shook his head. He was as stumped as she was. He'd hoped that verbalizing what they already knew would trigger something.

And then, suddenly, it did. Sort of. "Who handled the funeral arrangements?" he asked.

"You mean the next of kin?" she asked, not sure what he was driving at.

"No." Davis shook his head. "I mean the funeral parlor. Do we know which funeral parlor held the viewing for all these women?"

Offhand, Moira had no idea. "How would that tie in?"

"I'm not sure yet," Davis admitted. That didn't change the fact that he had a feeling that just maybe they were onto something. "But let's tackle one question at a time."

Moira grabbed her jacket off the back of her chair, ready to roll. "Sounds good to me," she said, preceding Davis out the door.

Because neither one of them knew the name— or names—of the funeral parlors where the bodies of the five deceased had been prepared for viewing, they were forced to go first to St. Joseph's Cemetery to talk to Weaver and then to Aurora's First Cemetery to see Campbell. Both had to have—or know where they could obtain—the necessary information.

First on their list, Weaver looked less than happy

to see them again. Resentful fear was very evident in the groundskeeper's demeanor. When the man discovered that all they wanted was the name of the funeral parlor that had handled the arrangements for the four dead women whose graves had been disturbed, he was more than happy to provide the information.

A quick search turned up the names of three different funeral parlors. Handing over the names and addresses—all three were still in business—Weaver quickly and joyfully ushered the two detectives out of the cemetery's business office.

Davis glanced over his shoulder at the departing lumbering figure. "You know, if I was inclined to be sensitive, I'd say that Weaver was trying to get rid of us," he told Moira as they got back to his car.

"Lucky for you that you've got a heart made of stone," Moira responded with a straight face.

"Lucky," Davis echoed, silently wondering if that was the word or even the case. His heart certainly hadn't felt all that solid during the weekend they had spent together.

Campbell, the second groundskeeper, provided them with the name of the funeral parlor that had been used for the deceased in his cemetery. It matched one of the names Weaver had given them.

So much for hoping the deceased had a funeral parlor in common, Davis thought. "Okay, I guess that didn't exactly pan out," he commented dourly as he got into his car again.

Moira slid in on the passenger side, chewing on

her lower lip and thinking. "Wait, don't rule it out yet. Maybe you were onto something, after all."

He didn't see how. "What are you getting at?" he asked. "They don't have a funeral parlor in common. There're three different ones."

"Agreed," she conceded. "But there still might be something that they did have in common."

Maybe it was his lack of sleep, but he wasn't following her. "Does this get any clearer?" he asked.

Her mind was going a mile a minute. "We need to go to these funeral homes and get a list of their employees for the last twenty years."

She was obviously onto something even if she wasn't being very clear about it.

He curbed his impatience. "What are you thinking?"

She looked up from the pages in her hand. He would have had to have been blind to have missed the excitement in her eyes. They were literally sparkling—and completely compelling, he couldn't help thinking.

He *really* needed to get his sleep.

"That maybe there was someone. A part-time employee…I don't know, maybe a salesclerk or a janitor—" Moira cast around, trying to solidify her thoughts, which were all over the board. "Just someone who worked in all three funeral homes that might be our connection."

It was obvious that she knew there was still a piece missing. "What are you not telling me?" he asked.

Still trying to organize her thoughts, she looked

at Davis. "What makes you think I'm holding something back?"

He laughed shortly, finally starting up the vehicle. He assumed that they were returning to the precinct. If they weren't, she'd tell him fast enough. "Because you look like a cat who's just found out about a train full of cream that's being shipped cross-country right through its backyard. Now talk."

"This isn't a competition," she pointed out, not wanting him to think she was deliberately withholding information.

"Everything's a competition with you."

Busted, Moira blew out a breath. "I just don't want to look like an idiot if I'm wrong."

"The idiot card is off the table," he promised her. "Now, what do you know?" Davis repeated.

Moira shifted in her seat, excitement slipping through her body as she spoke. "I did some background research into twenty-year-old news stories... Twenty-*one* years ago, Aurora had its biggest bank robbery on record. They caught one of the guys responsible, the other guy was killed," she recounted. "The money, however, was never found.

"Think about it," she urged, talking increasingly faster. "What better way to hide the money than to split it up and hide it in the coffins of five different people? All you need is a man on the inside to hide it under the lining."

Making a right at the next corner, Davis rolled the idea around for a moment. "Interesting theory," he agreed then spared her a quick glance. "How do we go about proving it?"

"Old-fashioned police legwork," she told him.

Davis pressed his lips together, stifling a yawn. "Give me the address of the first funeral home and let's go for it."

The directors at two of the funeral homes were very willing to comply with Moira's request. The third director offered his apologies, but insisted on a search warrant all the same.

Several hours passed before they returned, armed with the necessary paperwork. The director dutifully surrendered copies of the funeral home's personnel records.

Armed with the list of employees from all three, they finally returned to the precinct and went over all the names and other pertinent information in the files.

There was no match. All the employee names differed from one another.

Frustrated, wanting to throw something against a wall just to hear it smash, Moira angrily pushed the papers aside on her desk and banged her fist on the table. Her coffee cup fell over. Luckily, it was empty.

"Damn it," she cried. "I was so sure…"

"Maybe there's something else," Davis said, trying to stem her flash of temper despite the fact that he was experiencing a great deal of frustration himself.

"Like what?" she demanded hotly. "We've gone over everything that's possible!"

Moira scooped the employee lists up off the table,

fighting the urge to rip the pages in two. Instead, they slipped out of her hands, falling to the floor.

Muttering under her breath, she bent to pick them up.

That was when she saw it.

"Davis, look at this," she cried, almost jumping to her feet.

She poked a finger at the crucial fact that had caught her eye. Moira was almost afraid to hope, but this very well could be the break she and Davis were searching for.

Getting up, he came over to join her, looking at the paper she was holding. "Look at what?"

"Look at the makeup artists the funeral parlors use."

Davis examined the names she was singling out. All three funeral parlors used women, which in itself, he knew, didn't seem unusual.

"What about them?" he asked. "The names are all different."

It stunned her how stupid, or careless, criminals could actually be—and she almost hadn't noticed.

"Yes," she agreed, "the names aren't the same— but the social security numbers are." The next moment she was on the phone to Valri. The second her sister picked up on the other end, Moira started talking. "Last favor, I promise."

Davis could hear her sister answer. "Moira, I'm in the middle of something," the younger Cavanaugh protested wearily.

"I know, but this could be the break we've been looking for in the cemetery case," Moira stressed.

"Nine numbers. That's all I need you to look up. Just nine numbers. And I'll never bother you again."

Valri laughed. "Right. Until the next time," she said knowingly. "Okay, give them to me quickly," she ordered.

Once Moira read them to her, Valri hung up.

After five minutes had passed, Davis looked at her. "She's taking a long time. Maybe she can't get to it yet," he suggested.

Moira was having a hard time not fidgeting. "She'll get to it. I know Val. She'll get to it." She jumped as her phone rang.

"Yes?" she cried rather than give the official greeting she normally said when she answered the phone.

"I'm sending you the corresponding DMV photo linked to that social security number," Valri told her. Then, not waiting for a response, Valri declared, "I've gotta go," and quickly hung up.

"We've got it," Moira announced. She held up her cell phone for Davis to see a DMV facsimile of a Sylvia Elliot, a woman, Moira thought, who was one of Aurora's less than brilliant robbery accomplices. It was also the name of the woman who worked at Ames & Son Funeral Home, the second funeral parlor they'd visited.

Moira had a strong feeling that both Jane Andrews and Barbara Allen, the names of the other two makeup artists, would also respond to being called Sylvia.

"Okay, let's see if we can find which funeral home Sylvia—or whatever her real name is—is operating in today," she said.

Two phone calls later—after asking if the "lady

who makes the dearly departed look so lifelike" was there—Moira smiled triumphantly as she ended her call.

"She's working at Ames & Son Funeral Home." Glancing at her watch, she added, "We'd better hurry. It's getting late and 'Sylvia' just might decide to knock it off for the day—or forever if she's gotten what she was after."

"What are you thinking?" Davis asked as they hurried down the stairwell and out of the building to his car. "That she was part of the robbery and hid the money in the coffins of the people she was making look lifelike?"

"That's the general idea," she told him, pulling open the passenger door. It was beginning to feel as if she lived in his car.

"But in that robbery you talked about, according to the archives I just Googled, there were only two robbers. The one who was killed and the one who was sent to prison to do time." Buckling up, Davis started his vehicle.

"Maybe she wasn't there in person," Moira conceded, "but that doesn't mean she wasn't a wife or a girlfriend or maybe a cousin to one of the robbers. She could have been persuaded to hide the money until the heat was off."

"Or she could have driven the getaway car," Davis suggested as they pulled out of the lot.

Moira grinned as she nodded. "There's that, too. Lots of ways to tie an accomplice in—but first we have to make sure she *is* an accomplice and that I'm not just grasping at straws."

"Three aliases with the same social security number," Davis said, reiterating the point that she had initially raised. "I don't think that's a straw. That, Detective Cavanaugh, is the smoking gun."

"Amen to that," Moira said, crossing her fingers.

Chapter 19

Anticipation undulated through Moira as she came
through the front door of Ames & Son Funeral Home.
She had a gut feeling they were finally on the right
track to getting the answers to this puzzle that had
bedeviled her from the beginning.

No longer standing on ceremony, Moira dispensed
with any preliminary chitchat as she flashed her badge
at the funeral home director—just in case it had slipped
the man's mind that she and Davis represented the police department.

"Is your makeup artist still here, Mr. Ames?" she
asked.

Jon Ames, the grandson of the original Ames whose
name was on the sign outside the building, was a
somber-looking man who appeared as if he had stepped

out of central casting expressly for the role of morti-
cian. He seemed somewhat taken aback by her abrupt
question.

"You're the one who just called a few minutes ago,"
he realized, making the connection.

"And now we're here," Davis said pointedly. "The
detective asked you a question, Mr. Ames. It's impo-
lite not to answer."

"She's in the preparation room, but she's about to
go home," Ames told them, flustered. "What is this
all about?"

"My guess is about ten to twenty," Moira answered
flatly. "Which way to the preparation room?"

Still apprehensive, the funeral director pointed
down the hall.

"Jordan can show you the way," he volunteered, indicating the janitor.

The man was over in a corner, moving a carpet
sweeper back and forth across roughly the same spot
on the rug. Moira realized she hadn't even noticed the
nondescript man as she had walked in. He seemed to
just blend into the background.

"Jordan?" the director called, raising his voice.
"Would you show the detectives where the preparation room is?"

The thin, bald man leaned the carpet sweeper against
the wall and came forward. "Sure thing," he murmured.
Moving ahead of them, he said, "Follow me."

The janitor had a limp. Moira felt badly about putting the man out like this.

"Just tell us which room it is. I don't want to take you away from your work," she told him.

The janitor laughed shortly. "You're doing me a favor," he assured her. Reaching the room, he opened the door and stood back to allow them to enter. "Someone here to see you, Ms. Elliot."

The small, dark-haired woman getting her purse out of the small, narrow closet looked startled as she abruptly turned around. Her eyes swept over the janitor first then shifted to the two people who had entered the room ahead of him.

"Can this wait?" she asked, slipping the strap of her purse onto her shoulder. She seemed to clutch it for strength. "I'm in kind of a hurry."

"Got a plane to catch?" Moira asked amicably. The smile on her lips did not reach her eyes.

The woman she was addressing seemed exceedingly agitated and uncomfortable. "What?" The next moment her confusion seemed to lift and she answered. "No. Actually I—"

"Actually," Moira interjected, commandeering the word the makeup artist had started with. "You need to come with us."

The woman referred to as Sylvia looked from one detective to the other, her head almost swiveling as she did so.

"Where?" she asked defensively.

"Down to the precinct. We have a few questions for you," Davis told her.

"Can't you ask them here?" Sylvia asked, her tone

growing more and more agitated with each passing second.

"I'm afraid not," Moira told her. She debated taking handcuffs out then decided against it—as long as the woman came along peacefully. "It'll be easier for everyone all around if you just come with us now. With any luck, we can have this all cleared up in a couple of hours, Sylvia." She paused for a moment before asking the woman, "Or would you rather I call you Jane…or maybe Barbara?"

Fear entered the woman's hazel eyes. "There's been some mistake," she protested weakly.

Moira nodded, granting her the point. "And it was yours."

"No, it was yours."

The last words came from directly behind her. Swinging around, Moira saw that the janitor hadn't left the room. Instead he had pulled out a small handgun and was pointing the muzzle directly at her.

For a huge, pulsating moment, everything seemed to suddenly stop.

Sound became amplified.

She both heard and saw the man cock the gun's trigger.

Just like that, things were propelled forward, moving at a stomach-crunching, dizzyingly fast speed.

She heard Davis shout, "No! Not again! Not this time!" at the same time she felt his hand grab her arm as he yanked her away and pushed her behind him.

He was using his body to shield hers.

And then she saw him go down right in front of her. Blood was spurting everywhere.

Horrified, in shock, Moira shrieked, "No!" at the same time her training took over.

She didn't remember pulling out her own weapon; didn't remember firing it until the noise resounded in her ears. She saw the man who had shot Davis crumple to the floor, cursing at her.

Still clutching his weapon, the janitor tried to fire it at her, but Moira discharged her gun a split second before him.

The gun fell from his hand, useless, as shock and fury etched themselves into his pockmarked face— and remained there.

At the same time, Moira saw the woman begin to flee and she fired directly in front of her, stopping her dead in her tracks.

"Don't even think about it!" she ordered, keeping her weapon trained on Sylvia even as she sank to her knees beside Davis.

"Talk to me!" she begged him frantically. "Davis, talk to me!"

His eyes fluttered slightly as he struggled to open them. "Just…like a…woman," he whispered weakly. "Always…wanting to…talk at the…wrong…time."

The funeral director came scurrying in just then, apparently drawn by the gunfire. His eyes almost bugged out of his head as he looked around the room, clearly in shock.

"What happened?" he cried, stunned.

"Call 9-1-1," Moira ordered.

"But you're the police," Ames pointed out, bewildered.

"We need *more* police," she retorted. Pulling handcuffs out of her back pocket, she tossed them at the director. "Handcuff her!"

He'd barely caught the handcuffs and was staring at them as if they represented the mysteries of the universe. "I don't know—"

"Handcuff her!" Moira shouted again. "And call 9-1-1. Tell them we need an ambulance like five minutes ago!"

Finally snapping to life, Ames quickly complied with both orders.

The makeup artist cursed a blue streak at both her and the funeral director as the cuffs were closed around her wrists.

Moira was barely aware of what the man was doing. Every ounce of her being was focused on Davis. Completely focused on keeping him alive.

She was attempting to staunch the flow of blood coming from his chest wound; she only had her hands to use. Moira was furiously blinking back angry, frightened tears.

"Damn it, Davis, what the hell did you think you were doing?" Pale, he lay on the floor, unresponsive. Her breath solidified in her throat. "Davis? Davis!"

"Couldn't…lose…another…partner" was all he was able to say before he passed out.

The ambulance and backup from the precinct arrived at the same time.

Moira grabbed the handcuffed woman and pushed

her toward the first officer to walk through the door, struggling to curb her temper.

"Take her to the precinct and book her," she instructed tersely.

"What are the charges?" the police officer, Jim Daily, asked.

"Call the Chief of Ds," Moira told him. "Tell him we just solved our graveyard cold case. I'll call him with an update when I can." She had no more time to waste on the woman.

The paramedics had strapped Davis to the gurney and were transporting him out of the funeral home. "I've got to go," she told the officer. With that, she hurried after the gurney.

She stood to the side as the paramedics loaded Davis into the back of the ambulance, but the moment the gurney was in, she climbed inside.

"Detective," the paramedic riding in the back protested, "there's no room."

Moira wasn't about to leave Davis's side. She made it clear that the only way the paramedics were getting her off the ambulance was to push her out.

"I'm small. I won't breathe. I'll fit," she told him, leaving no room for argument.

The paramedic, whose badge read Eric, regarded her for a moment. "Cavanaugh?" he asked.

Moira unconsciously squared her shoulders, bracing herself for a confrontation. "Yes."

He sighed, nodding. "It figures. They warned me about you people." Craning his neck so that his voice carried to the front of the ambulance, Eric called out to his partner. "She's coming with us, Jeff. Let's go."

Moira took hold of Davis's hand. It felt almost clammy to the touch. What did that mean? She was afraid to think, afraid to live beyond the moment. Because the next moment might not have Davis in it.

"You hang in there, you hear me?" she said sharply, bending closer to his ear. "I'm not having this go down on my record. You're going to live, Gilroy. Understand? Like it or not, you're my partner and there's no escaping that. You're going to live! I'm not giving you permission to die."

She wasn't certain, but she thought she felt just the lightest squeeze from his hand. Maybe it was just her imagination, but she clung to that, and to him, the entire ride to the hospital.

Eight minutes felt like an eternity.

Moira only let go of her partner's hand after the ambulance had come to a stop and the paramedics had to take the gurney out of the ambulance. The minute the gurney's legs were snapped into place, she jumped out of the vehicle and took his hand in hers again.

She held it as they went through the inner electronic doors, down the corridor and to a private exam room within the ER.

A powerful-looking veteran nurse seemed to materialize out of nowhere. She put herself between Moira and the door leading into the exam room.

"You're not allowed in there," she insisted. "That's a restricted area and it's for hospital personnel only."

Frustrated beyond words, Moira glared at the

woman. "Then either give me a job or get out of my way!" she ordered.

The next moment, since the nurse was too stunned to answer her, Moira pushed her way past the speechless woman and went into the small, antiseptic room where a team of doctors and nurses, utilizing noisy monitors and the latest technology, were frantically working over Davis.

Grabbing a surgical mask on her way in, Moira covered her nose and mouth and positioned herself outside the circle of surgical personnel.

Moira struggled to keep the tears from falling.

"You don't belong in here," one doctor said when he noticed her, tossing the words over his shoulder as he worked on Davis. The statement was said between the orders he issued to the staff as he tried to stop the bleeding.

"I belong here just as much as you," she countered stubbornly in a small, emotional voice then promised, "I'll keep out of your way," as she bit back a sob.

Numb, Moira stood in a corner of the room, making herself as small as possible as she intently watched not the medical personnel working frantically over him, but Davis's chest as it rose and fell.

She willed it to keep on moving like that.

She didn't know just how long she had been standing there, watching and praying, willing Davis to live, before she felt someone from behind taking her by the elbow.

Thinking it was the nurse who'd tried to bar her

from entering earlier, Moira swung around, ready for a confrontation.

Spoiling for a fight.

Anything to drain this tense, helpless feeling that had taken her over.

"I'm *not* leaving," she declared stubbornly.

But instead of the heavyset nurse with the frown that was set in granite, Moira looked up into the sympathetic eyes of the Chief of Detectives.

"I know how you feel, Moira, but you can't be in here," he told her gently, his voice low. "Let the doctors here do their work. They've patched up more than half the force over the last couple of decades. They know what they're doing."

Suddenly, Moira had to struggle to keep from collapsing against her uncle, as if every bone in her body had turned to pudding.

"The nurse sent for you?" she heard herself asking. Her head was spinning as fear kept a stranglehold on her heart.

"No. Officer Daily called me about your collar," he told her, referring to one of the officers on the scene at the funeral parlor. "He filled me in as best he could about the shooting. I figure you'll give me the details when you can."

At the sound of her uncle's calm, rational voice, something she had been trying so hard to hold together just broke open inside Moira.

"That should have been me in there," she cried. The tears just kept coming and she couldn't stop them. "Davis pushed me out of the way and took the bullet meant for me." She raised her eyes to Brian's. "Why didn't I realize it?" she asked, angry with herself. "I should have realized it."

She was babbling now, but Brian acted as if she were making perfect sense, allowing her release as he slowly tried to piece what she was saying together. "Realized what?" he asked her gently.

"The janitor *limped*." She saw that her words meant nothing to her uncle. Why should they? They had meant nothing to her at first.

"That first morning, those two figures dressed in black running out of the cemetery collided with me. One of them must've gotten hurt worse than the other one because I remember seeing him limp as he ran off.

"The janitor took us to a room at the funeral home and *he* was limping. *He* was one of the two people at the cemetery, digging up that grave." She covered her mouth to keep the sob from escaping. "Why didn't I realize it?" she cried again.

"Being able to see all angles of everything isn't always possible," Brian told her. "The best we can do is just try to survive from one day to the next." Brian squeezed her shoulder, as if to offer her his strength. "Davis is strong, he'll survive," he told her firmly.

She knew he couldn't make a promise like that, but she didn't care.

She clung to it anyway.

Word spread quickly. Within the half hour, the hall was thick with law-enforcement agents, police officers and detectives alike. The medical staff, especially the nurses, at Aurora Memorial had learned to deal with the influx. A few of the newer ones, filled with commitment to their oath, attempted to herd the law-enforcement agents into rooms designated for the purpose of housing those who waited for news. The more experienced personnel knew it was easier threading the proverbial camel through the equally proverbial eye of a needle than it was to get police brethren and relatives to gather in some semblance of order.

They let them mill around wherever they chose. Most lined the halls outside the operating room.

To placate the hospital staff, Rose and Lila, the wives of Andrew and Brian respectively, came to the ER bearing warm cinnamon rolls. The number was on a scale that could have fed the masses gathered to hear the Sermon on the Mount. The gesture went a long way to smooth hurt feelings and also to fill the empty stomachs of those who waited.

Moira, now surrounded by her brothers and sisters as well as her extended family, ate nothing. All she did was watch the operating room door where they had taken Davis. Watched it and prayed as time simultaneously stood still and somehow managed to drag by, as well.

"How are you doing, kid?" Malloy, the last to arrive, asked.

She looked at him, her face and voice completely drained. "Ask me that when they wheel him into Recovery."

Malloy exchanged looks with Valri and Kelly. They all knew their sister meant it. Her existence and mental well-being all hung on Davis's condition when he came out of surgery.

Or *if* he came out of surgery.

Chapter 20

"Here."

Brian Cavanaugh handed his grandniece a smartphone before taking a seat beside her in Davis's hospital room. Close to twenty hours had passed since the latter had been rushed to the hospital for surgery. The detective, he'd been told, had yet to open his eyes.

And Moira, the chief was willing to bet, had yet to close hers. Though she was doing her best to disguise it, she was worried as well as tired.

Caught off guard, Moira looked at her granduncle and then at the smartphone he'd handed her. It was on, but the screen was dormant.

"What's this?" she asked.

"Well, I know you would have wanted to interrogate the woman you arrested in person," Brian explained.

"By the way, she actually does go by the name of Sylvia Elliot," he interjected before continuing with his explanation. "But I also know from experience that Cavanaugh women cannot be dynamited away from the bedside of someone they care about if that someone has just been on the wrong end of a bullet.

"So, in the interest of fair play and closure—after all, you *were* the one who pressed for this investigation to be undertaken in the first place—I brought the interrogation to you. We filmed it," he told her, "with the suspect's full understanding and knowledge that it was being filmed," he added, just so that there was no question of impropriety.

"Once she realized that her brother, the janitor, was dead, she was more than happy to try to pin everything that had happened—now and twenty-one years ago—on him, saying he forced her to do everything."

Moira shook her head. She was trying to follow what the chief was telling her, but her general lack of sleep, not to mention the fact that Davis still wasn't out of the woods, made her feel as if her brain was slightly scrambled.

"I'm sorry, Chief," she apologized. "My head feels a little foggy. I'm not really sure what you're telling me."

Brian smiled sympathetically. She'd been through a lot and no one knew it better than he did.

"The whole interrogation is all there, on the smartphone. You hold on to it and play it later, when you feel you can fully take it in. But the gist of it is, you were right," he told her with a satisfied smile.

"There *was* money hidden in those five caskets. Syl-

via's brother, Dean, and a friend of his, Mike Calderon, pulled off the bank robbery twenty-one years ago.
Calderon was killed and her brother didn't want to be
caught with the money, so he gave it to Sylvia to bury.

"Turns out he *was* caught, arrested and convicted.
The sentence was for thirty years, but he got out in
twenty for good behavior. You can figure out the rest
of it—actually, you *did* figure out the rest of it."

Finished, Brian looked over at Davis and then back
at her again. "I suppose it won't do any good to tell
you to go home. That someone from the hospital will
contact you the second he wakes up."

Moira merely shook her head. "No."

Brian laughed to himself. "I didn't think so." Even
so, he'd had to try. "Well, I just wanted to drop that
off with you," he told her, indicating the smartphone.

Brian rose to his feet. "Good job, Detective." His
eyes shifted toward Davis. "Both of you," he added.

Moira forced a smile to her lips. "Thank you, sir.
I'll be sure to tell him when he wakes up."

Brian nodded. He decided to give it one last try.
Stubbornness was not the exclusive province of the
younger generation. He was, after all, a Cavanaugh.
"At least try to grab a catnap, Detective."

"I'll do my best, sir," Moira promised, settling back
in her chair.

"You always do," Brian told her, making no effort
to hide the pride that he felt for the detective she had
become.

With that, he closed the door behind him as he left
the hospital room.

Moira slipped the smartphone the chief had given her into her pocket and shifted again in the chair, doing her best to get more comfortable.

Maybe if she just closed her eyes for a second, as he had suggested, she could grab a few winks and ultimately feel a little more like herself.

Stretching her legs out in front of her, Moira sighed and closed her eyes.

"Is he gone?"

Moira's eyes flew open, certain that she'd imagined the voice.

Imagined Davis talking to her. He hadn't regained consciousness yet.

Bolting upright, she looked at him, expecting to see Davis just as he'd been a moment ago, eyes closed and body inert.

His eyes were open.

"You're awake!" Moira cried, stunned, relieved and overjoyed all at the same time. It took everything she had to restrain herself from hugging him, but she was afraid of loosening one of the IV tubes.

It was obvious that he was still rather weak, but he was conscious. "Uh-huh."

"How long have you been awake?" she asked in disbelief.

As best as he could piece it together, the sound of the chief's voice, talking to Moira, had seeped into his consciousness by degrees, rousing him.

"I heard what the chief said," he told her. "At least most of it, I think."

"Then why didn't you say anything?" she asked.

He tried to shrug and found the various lines and monitors attached to him prevented him from doing so.

"I wasn't up to talking, at least not to anyone official."

"But you're up to talking to me?" she asked, trying to make sense of what he was saying.

"With you, all I'm doing is listening," he told her, his speech still a bit labored. The corners of his mouth curved ever so slightly.

When she thought of what had happened at the funeral home, what *could* have happened if Davis hadn't gotten to the hospital in time, her stomach twisted into a huge knot. He could have died because of that one reckless action.

Emotions close to the surface, she lashed out at him in anger. "What the hell were you thinking?" she demanded as wave after wave of terrifying thoughts washed over her, almost making her break down.

"Saving your life comes to mind," Davis answered weakly.

"By doing what? Sacrificing your own?" she retorted hotly. Didn't he understand what that would have done to her? Didn't he care about her just a little? On her feet now beside the bed, she fisted her hands impotently at her sides. "Oh, God, I could just beat on you!"

The knowing smile that slipped over his lips just fueled her frustrated anger. "You wouldn't hit a man when he's down."

"For you, I'd make an exception," she snapped. "Just who the hell do you think you are? Superman?"

Davis looked at her as if her question had sparked

a revelation. "You mean I'm not?" His voice sounded raspy as he asked, "What am I going to do with all those red capes?"

"How about if I strangle you with them?" she suggested. She felt as if she'd just fallen into an emotional blender, wanting to laugh and cry at the same time.

The closest look to innocence she'd ever seen on Davis crossed his face. "Have you always been this violent?"

"No," she snapped. "You just bring out the worst in me."

He smiled knowingly at her again. "Ditto," he responded.

And then it felt as if everything had been drained out of her: the anger, the fear, not to mention every last ounce of energy. She feathered her fingers along his face—at least there she couldn't disturb any tubes or monitors.

"Seriously, you shouldn't take chances like that," she told him. "You almost died."

His eyes met hers and she had never seen him looking this serious, this solemn. "If that lowlife had shot you, I would have," Davis said quietly. "I didn't want to lose you."

Words escaped her as she looked at him, stunned. Collecting herself, Moira took a breath and told him, "Don't worry, I won't hold you to that. That's just the painkiller talking. You probably won't even remember saying that tomorrow morning."

But she planned to hold that to her heart for the rest of her life, Moira silently told herself.

Davis tightened his fingers around hers, or tried to as best he could. "That's the painkiller *letting* me talk," he corrected.

He felt as if a barrier had been lifted, taken out of the way, allowing his feelings to take possession of him. Allowing him to express those feelings to the woman who had somehow, through her dogged perseverance, made him remember that he still *had* feelings, even though they had been held in abeyance for so long he'd forgotten about their existence.

Embarrassed for going on that way, he changed the subject. "So, we got 'em, huh?"

Moira beamed at him, still holding on to his hand. "We got 'em," she echoed.

And then something occurred to him. "I guess that means we're not partners anymore."

She hadn't thought of that. The deal had been that he was on loan for the duration of the investigation. Now that the case was solved, there was no need for him to stick around.

No need for them to be partners.

Unless…

"That all depends," she intoned after a moment of frantic calculation.

"On what?" he asked, puzzled.

Davis realized he was more than willing to be up for anything she had in mind. He didn't want to see their partnership dissolve. At least, if they were working together, he had an excuse to see her on a regular basis. He didn't want that to end.

"Is there an opening in Major Crimes?" she asked him out of the blue.

"Why? Are you thinking of switching?" Though he would have welcomed having her, that didn't make any practical sense to him. "You just solved a major cold case for your department."

"Exactly—and I did it by going over the lieutenant's head after he told me to drop the investigation. No matter how toothy his grin gets over the plus in his Solved column, he's going to have it in for me for 'showing him up.' The man is petty like that," she told Davis as she pulled the chair closer to his bed and sat again. "It's not an atmosphere I like working in…

"Your captain seems like an okay guy without an ax to grind. If there is an opening in your department, I think I could talk my way into it."

Davis laughed and immediately pressed a hand against his chest.

"Damn, that hurts," he confessed then quickly collected himself before she got it into her head to call for the doctor. He'd had enough of doctors for a while—and not enough of her. "You, Cavanaugh, could undoubtedly talk your way past the gates of heaven if you set your mind to it."

Moira pretended to take offense. "Are you telling me I wouldn't get there through merit?"

"No," he corrected, "I'm telling you that you probably wouldn't want to do it that way because it would seem too tame to you. You like a challenge."

Moira looked at him pointedly. "That I do," she assured him with a smile.

"So," she went on after a long moment, "you're okay if I apply for a transfer to Major Crimes?"

He'd thought he'd made his feelings about that— and her—clear. "Why wouldn't I be?"

"Well, since you said you didn't have a partner— didn't *want* a partner," Moira amended, "if I apply to your department and they take me, they might just partner us up."

"I'm okay with that," he assured her. "In case you haven't noticed, I broke the jinx." To emphasize his point, he touched the bandages over his wound.

"I noticed. Oh, God, I noticed," she assured him, struggling not to melt against him the way she sorely wanted to.

Because he was feeling a little better, Davis wanted a few answers while he could still process them. "What happened to that little weasel who shot me?" he asked. "Did you arrest him?"

"I shot him," she said flatly.

"Dead?" There was something about her expression that answered him before she did.

"Dead."

"Wow." He blew out a breath, sorry that he had missed her in action. She must have been something to see. "Remind me not to get you mad."

"Too late," she told him. "But there might be a way to avoid getting shot."

"Oh?"

She nodded her head as she tried to keep a straight face. "I'm open to negotiations."

Davis raised an eyebrow. "What kind of negotia-tions?"

"Close ones." On her feet again, she leaned over his bed and lightly brushed her lips against his.

"Oh, if they're going to be effective," he told her, "they're going to have to be closer than that."

She laughed, relieved and happier than she had been in a very long time. "When you get better, Gilroy," she promised.

His eyes emphasized the smile on his lips. "Then I'd better get better fast."

She knew she'd be counting the days. "My thoughts exactly."

Epilogue

"You know," Davis began, measuring each word slowly after attempting several false starts in his head first. "I've been thinking about our partnership."

It had been another long day on the streets and at the precinct, and they were finally driving home. True to her word, Moira had applied for—and gotten—a transfer to the major crimes division the minute that Davis had been released from the hospital.

He'd been partnered with her for a little more than six months now. Because of that, they were together at work every day and then also together after hours every night.

So far, it had been going well. Better than she had expected. But despite her upbeat, optimistic nature, Moira never took anything for granted. The nature of her work had taught her that life could change completely in a heartbeat.

And there was something in his voice that caught her attention and struck her as out of the ordinary.

"Oh?" Moira asked, trying to sound nonchalant. "What about it?"

They had used his car today, so consequently, he was the one driving. He didn't answer her immediately, waiting, instead, until he came to a stop at a light.

His mouth felt dry as he told her, "I think maybe it's time to take it a step further."

For all intents and purposes, they were already living together, although he hadn't given up his apartment yet. Most nights, however, they stayed at her condo. On occasion, his apartment. In the past six months, ever since she'd insisted on being his nurse until he was back on his feet again, they'd been together. As far as she could see, this was "further."

"Just what did you have in mind?" she asked, doing her best to keep the apprehension out of her voice, even though it was making her mouth dry.

"Well." He stretched out the word. "Christmas is coming."

That wasn't exactly a news bulletin. "I know that. It's on all the calendars."

"But I can't wait for Christmas," he confessed, speeding up to get through the next light.

They barely made it through.

This wasn't like him, she thought. Her apprehension grew.

"There's no way to hurry it," she told him, tensing as she waited for a shoe to fall or a hammer to drop. "Department stores have tried."

Suddenly he pulled over into a strip mall parking lot. Most of the stores were closed and the lot was close to empty. She had no idea what to expect.

"But I can hurry this," he told her. "I was going to save it to give you for Christmas, but it's burning a hole in my pocket."

"Davis, what are you talking about?" she asked. She'd never seen him this way. He was almost nervous. The Davis she knew didn't get nervous. Was he about to tell her that he wanted to break up their partnership?

"This." As he said the single word he opened his hand.

Moira stifled a squeal.

Her response brought a flash of relief to him. Maybe this was going to be all right, after all. "I didn't know you squealed."

"Not one of my better qualities," she admitted, unable to take her eyes off the sparkling, heart-shaped diamond ring in the palm of his hand. An overhead streetlight caught the diamond, making it gleam almost flirtatiously at her.

Her heart was hammering in her chest the same way it had the first time he'd kissed her.

"I'm not versed in 'squeal.' Does that mean yes or no?" he asked her. He felt naked and vulnerable, waiting for her answer.

Moira raised her eyes to his. "If you have to ask,

then maybe you're not nearly as bright as I thought you were. But you have to be smart, because I wouldn't be in love with you if you weren't smart," she admitted breathlessly.

"Wait, you love me?" he asked incredulously.

He looked almost stunned, she realized. "Isn't that what we're talking about? Love?" she asked. "Or have you just decided to start handing out engagement rings at random?"

"Of course I love you," he practically retorted. "It's that I just didn't think that you—I mean I wasn't sure—oh, the hell with it," he cried, slipping the ring on her finger.

"My sentiments exactly," she agreed, laughing just before he kissed her to seal the bargain.

It demanded a lot of sealing.

She didn't mind.

* * * * *

If you loved this novel, don't miss other
suspenseful titles by Marie Ferrarella:

COLTON COPYCAT KILLER
SECOND CHANCE COLTON
HOW TO SEDUCE A CAVANAUGH
CAVANAUGH FORTUNE

Available now from
Mills & Boon Romantic Suspense!

*For a sneak peek of
Marie's next Cavanaugh book,
CAVANAUGH COLD CASE,
turn the page...*

Prologue

Josephine Alberghetti placed an overly generous portion of lasagna in front of her daughter and then sighed as she sat opposite her.

"Mom, you've been sighing like that since I walked in through the door ten minutes ago. What's up?" Dr. Kristin Alberghetti asked her mother.

Her mother pressed her lips together, as if hesitating to give voice to what was fairly bursting to come out.

The next moment the hesitation was over.

At this point in her life Josephine saw no reason to stew over anything. She knew firsthand how fleeting life could be.

"When you first came to me and told me that you wanted to be a doctor, I was so proud I could have burst," Josephine told her only child. "I wasn't sure just how we were going to pay for it with your father, God rest his soul, gone, but I remember being so very, very proud. I was willing to work my fingers to the bone, putting in twenty hours a day to make my little girl's dream come true."

Kristin knew where this was going. The same place that it had gone before.

"Uncle Gasper lent you the money, Mom," Kristin reminded her mother patiently. "Actually he *gave* you most of it."

Though her father's uncle had fought her, she had stubbornly insisted on paying the man back. It hadn't been easy, but she'd done it, taking and holding down jobs whenever she could while going to medical school. Through extreme dedication and concentrated energy, she'd managed to graduate ahead of time, thanks to an accelerated program.

But this wasn't about her mother's sacrifices—of which there were a legitimate number. This was about something else.

And Kristin had a very strong feeling she knew what that "something else" was.

Kristin and her mother were seated at the table in the kitchen where she had spent her first seventeen years. She had only half an hour to spare and had actually popped in to visit in the middle of the morning—taking a couple of hours of personal time—because her mother had complained about being neglected. Feeling guilty, Kristin had juggled a few things, put a couple more on hold and then dashed over during her break.

Kristin's grandmother, Sophia, a fixture in her life

for as far back as she could remember, was also there. Kristin exchanged glances with her now. She knew what was coming, as did her grandmother. Out of respect for her mother—because she knew how frustrated Josephine Alberghetti was—Kristin kept her silence. But it wasn't easy.

"But why you took all that wonderful knowledge," Josephine was saying, "and training and practically just threw it out the window to become a medical examiner, poking around inside dead people, is really, *really* beyond me." She looked at her daughter pleadingly. "Can't you just go into private practice? Think of the good you could be doing."

"I *am* doing good, Mom," Kristin told her mother. This certainly wasn't the first time they had done this dance, but her mother seemed to refuse to remember that she felt she had good reasons to have chosen this route. She patiently repeated it. "I'm bringing closure to a great many families who need answers."

In response, Josephine rolled her hazel eyes dramatically. "Closure," she murmured under her breath as if it was a dirty word.

"Leave her alone, Josephina," Sophia told her daughter sharply. The family matriarch smiled at her granddaughter. "She is happy closing things. It is her life."

"And she's *wasting* it," Josephine retorted. "How is Kristin supposed to meet anyone when she's standing in the middle of a morgue, surrounded by dead people for heaven's sake?" she demanded.

"Did you not hear her?" Sophia asked, the volume of her voice increasing as she made her point. At nearly eighty, Sophia Moretti's voice was as strong and loud as when she'd first arrived in America at the age of twenty-eight. "She is closing things for families. Maybe one of those families has a son—"

Kristin stared at her grandmother, grappling with a sudden feeling of betrayal. No matter what, her grandmother had always been on her side. "You, too, Nonny?"

Sophia leaned over the food-laden kitchen table to pat her granddaughter's hand. "I am just trying to—how you say?—*humor* your mama. Marry, don't marry, it is all the same to me. Just be happy, Little One," she said to her youngest granddaughter. "The family has enough small people already."

"Easy for you to say." Josephine pouted, trying to keep the bitterness out of her voice. "*You* have lots of grandchildren and great-grandchildren."

Sophia pursed her lips together. "We are all family, Josephina. We share. You want some grandchildren? I will let you have some of mine."

"Listen to Nonny," Kristin coaxed. "We all live in Aurora. You need short people to hug, you can go over to Theresa's or Lorraine's or Angela's," she said, enumerating her cousins, all of whom were married with at least two if not more children, "and hug one of their kids."

"I love those children," her mother replied honestly. "But it's not the same thing and you know it," Josephine complained. She looked at her mother accusingly. "You're supposed to be on my side."

Sophia raised coarse hands that had been weathered by decades of hard work and pretended to push back her daughter's words of rebuke. "I take no sides. I just sit and listen."

To which Josephine replied a contemptuous, "Ha!"

Any response from her mother was interrupted by Kristin's cell phone. It was ringing.

Josephine sighed deeply as she watched her daughter reach into one of her pockets and take out the offending electronic gadget.

To Josephine, phones did not belong in pockets and they certainly didn't belong at a family meal. She'd been so pleased to see her daughter standing in the doorway, she'd forgotten to insist that Kristin shut off her phone.

Holding her hand up for momentary silence, Kristin listened to the call. Her boss, Sean Cavanaugh, the chief of the crime scene investigation lab was on the other end of the line.

"Sorry to interrupt your personal time, Doctor, but I'm afraid we need you at a crime scene," he told her, his deep voice rumbling in her ear. "We've found two bodies so far."

"So far?" Kristin repeated uncertainly, surprised at the way he'd phrased the news. "Are you expecting to find more?"

"Oh, yes," she heard him respond wearily. "It looks like there might be quite a few."

How many were there in "quite a few"? Kristin wondered, a shiver threatening to slide up and down her spine. "That sounds like you've hit some kind of mother lode, sir."

"That's what I'm afraid of," he told her. "I'd appreciate it if you got here as soon as you could."

"On my way," Kristin told him quietly.

Sophia lowered her voice as she leaned toward her daughter, taking care not to interfere with her granddaughter's call. "What means this 'mother lode'?" she whispered.

Josephine sighed as she rose to her feet and began to put away the food she had taken out the minute her daughter had walked through the door. Family mealtimes were treasured, no matter when they took place and how small the family unit at that particular moment might be.

She transferred Kristin's serving onto a paper plate, then quickly wrapped it all up in aluminum foil. "It means, Ma, that Kristin is leaving."

Chapter 1

It wasn't going to be one of his better days.

He could just feel it in his bones.

The road Malloy Cavanaugh was driving seemed almost dangerously hypnotic. He'd been on it for close to half an hour. His eyes felt as if they were burning—always a bad sign—and his eyelids kept threatening to shut on him. Thanks to the rather considerable charms of a young woman he'd met the other night with the not totally inaccurate nickname of Bunny, he had gotten very little sleep the past two nights.

Hence, Detective Malloy Cavanaugh was not his usual energetic self this morning.

Catching up on a backlog of paperwork would have been far more to his liking at this point. At least, if he fell asleep at his desk, there was no danger of driving that desk into a ditch or off the side of the inclined road the way there was at the moment.

Aurora, California, where he had moved several years ago with the rest of his family, was a work in progress; a city whose council worked hand in hand with its developers. Consequently—and aesthetically— that development progressed slowly.

What that ultimately meant was, according to his uncles, Aurora had taken thirty-five years to go from a rural, two-lane, three-traffic-light town to the major thriving city it was today.

That also meant that there were still large parcels of land that were generally undeveloped. Most of them were located on the outskirts of the southern perimeter of Aurora.

That was where he was traveling right now, on his way to a crime scene that, it seemed, had the dubious distinction of being both the site of a multiple homicide and the site of a cold case all at the same time. The bodies, according to the crime scene investigators who had been summoned by the first officer on the scene, had apparently been in the ground for years, the exact amount of time—as well as the exact number of bodies—had yet to be determined.

Hell of a way to start a Monday morning, Malloy thought, stifling a yawn before it managed to momentarily make him shut his eyes.

He took in a deep breath, trying hard to rouse himself. A better way to go would have been to drink some of the pitch-black, strong coffee riding next to him in his vehicle's cup holder, but unless he pulled over—

something, considering the narrowness of the winding road he was on, that was not advisable—he was not about to risk reaching for the tall container and bringing it to his lips.

For that to happen, the split second that his eyes might be off the road and on the container could just be enough to send him careening into an accident.

Notoriously happy-go-lucky and possessed of what some had referred to as a charmed life, Malloy was still not reckless enough to think himself above any and all accidents. Better safe than sorry had been an unspoken mantra in his family, courtesy of his very wise, late mother.

All things considered, he chose to obey it this morning.

The coffee could wait.

Instead, Malloy did his best to snap his countenance into alert wakefulness by biting down hard on the inside of his bottom lip. He stopped just short of drawing blood.

His eyes still burned. Just where the hell was this damn stupid nursery he was going to anyway? he wondered grudgingly.

According to the information he had been given just before he'd left the precinct, the bodies had been discovered by the owner of a construction company while clearing some unused land that belonged to the nursery. The idea was to extend the nursery and erect more greenhouses across two additional acres.

The greenhouse was to display even more specimens of cacti and succulents. As if four acres wasn't already enough, Malloy thought darkly.

At the age of eight, after running through what he thought was an empty field at twilight, he'd tripped and been almost impaled on the sharp, near-lethal spines of a small but menacing saguaro. Malloy had developed an aversion for everything and anything that even remotely looked as if it belonged to the cacti family.

To his mind, it only seemed natural that an aversion to succulents should follow, as well. Though a collector would argue the point, it seemed like one and the same to him.

He was vaguely aware that there were whole clubs devoted to meeting regularly and discussing the care and feeding of various species of these visually ugly plants, but for the life of him, he could not fathom why.

But then, he didn't understand why anyone would pay more than the cover price of a so-called rare comic book, either.

It took all kinds, Malloy told himself.

Taking a turn down yet another obscure road whose sign he had almost missed, Malloy breathed a sigh of relief. Apparently he was almost at journey's end. There was a sign posted up ahead just before a newly installed chain-link fence.

The sign proclaimed Rainbow Gardens. The sign looked new, as well.

According to what he'd been told, the old nursery, which had gone by—to his way of thinking—the far more accurate name of Prickly Gardens, had been sold a little more than a month ago. The present owner had come in with new ideas, the first of which had included expansion of the nursery so that even more plants could be properly showcased.

Sorry, no expanding yet, Malloy thought. There's the little matter of bodies to clear up.

Malloy pulled his car right up to the gate. The latter was closed.

There was another sign, an older, weathered one that told whatever traveler approached the gate that visitors were admitted By Appointment Only. It went on to say that if the visitor did have an appointment, to Please Honk.

There was what looked to be a trailer some distance away perched just above a row of several small greenhouses, not to mention a great many succulents and cacti that were in the ground and growing at a very prodigious rate.

Malloy assumed that honking was for the benefit of whoever was inside the trailer.

With his engine running as his car stood in front of the gate, Malloy paused to drain half the coffee in the container he'd brought. Only then did he do as the sign advised.

He honked his car's horn.

When there was no immediate response, Malloy did it again, this time leaning on his horn until he saw movement from the trailer.

A man wearing gray dress slacks and a crisp, long-sleeved, button-down blue shirt approached the gate. He appeared totally out of place in the rural-looking, overgrown nursery.

He also looked agitated.

Unlocking the gate, the man greeted Malloy by announcing, "Finally!" as he pulled it back.

Malloy drove down the slope and into the nursery, pulling his vehicle over to the first available parking area. The entire space meant, he assumed, to accommodate several vehicles, seemed barely wide enough to house three very compact cars.

Deliberately taking his time—he didn't care for the owner's attitude—Malloy stepped out of his car almost in slow motion, his shoes carefully making contact with the sun-cracked dirt.

Looking at the man who made no secret of sizing him up, Malloy said, "Excuse me?"

"I said 'finally.'" The man bit the word off sharply. "Maybe now that you're here, you can move this so-called investigation along." It wasn't a question but a strongly worded order. Angry, the man contemptuously indicated the four idle men in the distance. "That construction crew is being paid by the hour to stand around and watch that woman over there bend over."

Okay, maybe he'd had less than the minimum hours of sleep to be sufficiently operational, Malloy thought, but he had just had a really good jolt to his system thanks to the coffee he'd imbibed a minute ago and the scowling man in front of him *still* wasn't making any sense.

"You want to run that by me again?" Malloy requested. Then, before the man could say anything in response, he made clear what he wanted to hear first. "Starting with your name."

"I'm Roy Harrison," the man grudgingly declared. "And I just had my lawyer buy this property for me."

There was practically steam coming out of the man's rather large ears. In his position, Malloy supposed he wouldn't exactly be thrilled, either. "I take it congratulations are not in order."

"Damn straight they're not," Harrison snapped. "I paid for a cacti and succulent nursery, not some freaking boneyard," he growled in disgust. "Can't you and that former cheerleader take these damn bones and do whatever it is you have to do with them somewhere else? I've got a nursery to get ready to open," the man added unnecessarily.

"I'm afraid nothing's happening on that end until all the evidence is bagged and tagged and we can determine whether or not this was the actual scene of the crime—or if it was somewhere else." Though he kept his expression unreadable, Malloy rather enjoyed putting a pin in the man's balloon. He'd never cared for people who were filled with their own importance—especially unjustifiably.

The answer did not sit well with the new nursery owner. Harrison's scowl became almost fierce as he waved a hand angrily in Sean Cavanaugh's general direction. The latter was standing in the distance, working alongside his team.

"I overheard that old guy say that these bones have been in the ground for probably two decades. What the hell difference can it make where you look at them?" Harrison demanded. "They're old."

"It makes a great deal of difference," Malloy told

the new owner, his voice deceptively calm. "And that 'old guy' you just referred to happens to be my uncle and the head of the crime scene investigation lab," he added crisply, "so maybe you could find it in your heart to show a little respect for the man and his considerable knowledge. Who knows, you play your cards right and he actually might find a way to shorten the time lag."

Harrison already looked less than pleased to find himself stymied like this, not to mention being rebuked by someone he made quite obvious that he felt was beneath him.

The next moment Harrison took out his wallet, his implication clear as he tugged on a large-denomination bill. "What can I do to make this go faster?"

There was nothing but barely bridled contempt in Malloy's eyes now. "Not bribing me would be a good start." He flashed a completely phony smile at the offensive nursery owner. "Hang tight, Harrison, I'll have some questions for you." But he needed to check in with the CSI team first. "Now, about that 'former cheerleader' you mentioned—"

A barely veiled sneer curved Harrison's thin lips. "Let me guess, another relative?"

Malloy had just spotted the woman the owner had to be referring to. She was the only female in the area and from what he could see from this distance, whoever she was, she was nothing short of a breathtaking knockout.

All memory of the woman he'd spent the weekend with completely vanished.

"God, I hope not," Malloy commented under his

breath. "I'll get back to you," he added without sparing the owner a look.

"Who *can* I call to make this go away?" Harrison wanted to know, still not willing to surrender to the inevitable just yet.

"You don't," Malloy answered with finality, tossing the words over his shoulder.

Putting the abrasive owner temporarily out of his thoughts, Malloy made his way toward what was the only center of activity within the area—if he didn't count a neighbor's rooster.

The lone fowl was housed in an open coop facing the northern perimeter.

Flapping his wings and moving around in what could only be called an agitated manner, the rooster crowed intermittently despite the fact that the sun had long since been up and the current hour was quickly approaching noon.

Obviously the rooster's inner clock needed some adjusting, Malloy absently thought.

For the moment his attention was not on the rooster or the dead bodies that were the reason he had made his way out to this isolated area of Aurora in the first place. It was strictly and exclusively on the attractive woman who appeared to be totally absorbed by the bones she and two of the CSI agents were digging up out of the ground and arranging on a long, extended roll of cloth.

The annoying owner had been right, Malloy noted, scanning the immediate area. The construction crew he had hired was, for all intents and purposes, immobilized, no doubt ordered to remain that way by his uncle.

But the crew definitely didn't appear to be suffering any discomfort because of that edict.

Instead, the inert four men looked to be quite entertained as they took in every nuance, every movement, made by the young woman who was studying the various excavated bones that had been carefully spread out on the long length of sun-bleached cloth.

All thoughts of his exhausting night and the very agile, equally exhausting Bunny became a thing of the past at lightning speed.

Malloy approached the young woman and placed himself between her and the sunlight that had, until that moment, been highlighting the collection of bones she had been, and was, assembling.

"Hi, I'm Malloy," he told her.

The sudden, distracting shift of light caught her attention after several beats. A couple more passed before Kristin finally looked up.

If the exceedingly handsome, exceptionally confident-looking man momentarily threw her off her game, Kristin gave no indication of that reaction.

Instead her eyes met his and she silently waited for him to explain why he was blocking her light. His smile was wide, sexy and inviting. It wasn't something he had to practice; it just was.

The name he offered nudged at something in the back of her mind, coaxing bits and pieces of acquired and overheard information to come forward and form a whole. After a moment recognition began settling in.

Malloy Cavanaugh.

His reputation had preceded him.

"Of course you are," she replied, turning her attention back to her work.

"And you are?" he asked after a beat when she didn't volunteer her name once he had given her his.

"Busy," Kristin answered without looking up. "And you're in my light," she added impatiently.

"Funny, I would have thought that you cast enough light on your own to brighten up anything you needed to look at," Malloy told her.

She looked up then, her expression telling him that the remark—and his charm—left her more than just merely cold.

"Sorry, no," she replied. Ice chips formed around each word. "Would you mind stepping to the side? I got the impression that the owner of this nursery wanted me to be done before I even got here, so if you move out of the light, I can try to accommodate him."

"Sorry," Malloy apologized, following her request. "My bad."

"I imagine you probably say that a lot," Kristin commented, sounding as if she were saying that to herself instead of to him.

Feisty, Malloy thought.

Ordinarily he probably would have backed away. There was, after all, a case and he wasn't the type to waste too much time trying to break through a woman's barriers. For one thing, life was too short for that. For another, he was being paid to be a detective not a lover. And there were a great many willing women out there to choose from.

But, on the other hand, there was a certain appeal to the concept of "feisty," especially when it was coupled with someone who looked the way this woman did.

Who was she?

What was her official position in the department and how did he get her to open up to him?

"You're new," he said, hoping to initiate a conversation.

Kristin spared him just the minutest of glances before she went back to her work. "Actually, I'm not," she told him.

"I haven't seen you around," he told her. "And I always notice beautiful women."

"Well, I guess you missed one this time," she responded, carefully separating two bones that looked as if they had been fused together by time.

Rather than get annoyed, the flippant way she'd answered what was clearly a line—he hadn't been trying to be subtle—seemed to oddly attract him to an even greater extent.

Crouching beside her, he said, "Let's start over."

The look she gave him would have withered a lesser man.

"Maybe later. I'm working now." Her expression turned impatient. "And you're in my light again."

"Right."

To accommodate her, Malloy rose, taking care to allow the sunlight to stream over and bathe the bones laid out for her.

This one, he told himself, was going to be a tough nut to crack.

And he couldn't wait to get started.

MILLS & BOON®

Helen Bianchin v Regency Collection!

40% off both collections!

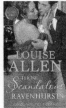

0316_MB520

MILLS & BOON®

INTRIGUE
Romantic Suspense

A SEDUCTIVE COMBINATION OF DANGER AND DESIRE

A sneak peek at next month's titles...

In stores from 7th April 2016:

- **The Marshal's Justice** – Delores Fossen *and*
  Allegiances – Cynthia Eden
- **Roping Ray McCullen** – Rita Herron *and*
  Urgent Pursuit – Beverly Long
- **Tribal Law** – Jenna Kernan *and*
  Smoke and Ashes – Danica Winters

Romantic Suspense

- **Conard County Spy** – Rachel Lee
- **Her Colton P.I.** – Amelia Autin
